RIDING JUDGMENT TRAIL

Maritza,

Enjoy your trail ride
through the old Southwest!

Best wishes —
Diane

Also by DIANE M. CECE

Available from Xlibris LLC

Riding Judgment Trail

(Book 6 in the Southwest Trails Series)

Flying T2 Brand

Diane M. Cece

Library of Congress Control Number:		2016908943
ISBN:	Hardcover	978-1-5245-0631-5
	Softcover	978-1-5245-0630-8
	eBook	978-1-5245-0629-2

Print information available on the last page.

Rev. date: 06/06/2016

To order additional copies of this book, contact:
Xlibris
1-888-795-4274
www.Xlibris.com
Orders@Xlibris.com
738969

CONTENTS

DEDICATION

Joan-Marie, Doug, Jim, Winnie, Steve, JoAnn,
Bill, Nancy, Carole Ann and Carroll

Only my brothers and sisters know me better than I know myself. It is a comfort to know we can count on each other through thick and thin, and whatever life brings on; and bring it on, it did. Thanks to you all for being there.

Acknowledgements

The author would like to take this opportunity to thank several individuals from without whose assistance this series could not have been possible.

Thank you Mary Flores, Publishing Consultant; Kris Alberto, submissions representative; Lani Martin, and Clifford Young, author services representatives; James Colonia, Lloyd Griffith, Cynthia Mathews, and Neil Reid, manuscript services representatives; Marly Trent, Orlando Wade, Rey Flores, Rafael Servado, marketing service representatives; Tony Hermano, author consultant; Lloyd Baron, web design; Amerie Evans, senior book consultant; Rye Lawrence marketing consultant, and Leo Montano, customer services.

Thank you John Covert, 27thnewjerseycompanyf.org, for designing my website dianesoldwestnovels.com. John you have been a tremendous inspiration for getting this author technologically advanced.

Thanks again everyone for being a part of my life and my work, you are the best ever that anyone can have available at their right side as colleagues and friends.

Nevada Kid's Family Tree

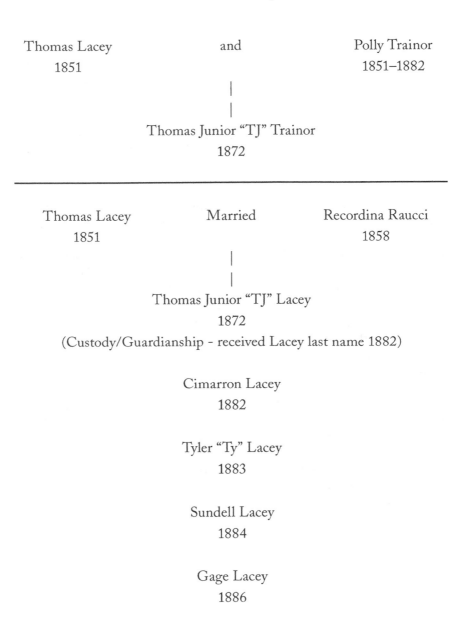

| Thomas Lacey
1851 | and | Polly Trainor
1851–1882 |

Thomas Junior "TJ" Trainor
1872

| Thomas Lacey
1851 | Married | Recordina Raucci
1858 |

Thomas Junior "TJ" Lacey
1872
(Custody/Guardianship - received Lacey last name 1882)

Cimarron Lacey
1882

Tyler "Ty" Lacey
1883

Sundell Lacey
1884

Gage Lacey
1886

Chapter I

WAKEUP CALL

I opened my eyes to the flickering of the sunshine on them, and the only thing I knew was that I had a gosh-awful bad headache. My pillow was a large boulder so whatever happened, I realized I must have hit my head on the rock it was resting on when I fell---if that is what happened, if I fell.

I moved my arms, and they seemed to be fine; no pain there. When I moved my legs, they felt quite stiff; however, they loosened up and moved freely and seemed to be okay also. No broken bones in my extremities. I sat up, and my head began to spin and reel like a child's toy top so I held on to the rocks jutting out of the wall next to me. The spinning and reeling slowed down and stopped. My back seemed to be okay, a little sore from the fall, but it too hurt with a few sore muscles at the most.

When I looked to my left side, all I could see was the rock wall of a mountain going straight up. It's when I looked to my right side that I shot the cat over the ledge and lost almost everything that was in my belly from the day before. I was sitting on a ledge that jutted out on the side of a mountain. There was nothing underneath that ledge but the rock wall of the mountain going straight down into a ravine forty feet below. I looked at the rock where my head was, and it had some sticky blood on it. When I felt around my head wound, there was dry blood on it in an open cut or gash where I hit it on the rock. This was definitely not good. It is a wonderment the dried blood stopped the wound from bleeding out and killing me.

How I got on this ledge I had no clue, and this ledge I estimated to be at the least forty feet in the air above the ravine. The ravine below was deep with jagged cuts in the rocks daring me to come down and try my luck at surviving by descending the mountainside. There would be no climbing back up that rock wall to the trail above, since it was way too steep. My best bet to get off this mountain ledge was to climb down it to what looked like the lower part of the trail and a meandering brook or was it a river alongside that trail. It was hard to tell from this high up. There was no question about it, I had to get down to the lower trail and get a drink of that cold moving water if I wanted to survive.

That's when I saw the dead horse at the bottom of the ravine. The horse must be mine, and we must have fallen off the trail that wound down the side of the mountain from way up above. When my horse hit this ledge on its way down, it must have thrown me onto the ledge saving my life, but my horse didn't live through the fall. The gelding must have tumbled down the mountainside bouncing somersaults down into the ravine and stopping against that stand of trees it was leaning against. The buzzards were already cutting circles in the air around the poor animal.

My saddle, my gear, and everything I owned were on that dead horse, and the buzzards were ready to dive out of the sky and enjoy a feast. I had no choice but to climb down the side of this rugged mountain and get to my stuff. Whatever I could salvage was important for my survival. I picked my gun up out of the dirt where it fell and returned it to my holster.

I slowly and carefully guided my footsteps and was able to slip down the side of the mountain like a snake slithering over some rocks. When I reached the bottom safely I sat down to catch my breath because I felt exhausted. For some reason my head did not feel like it was attached to my body. It felt like I was swinging in outer space sort of like Orion hanging suspended and motionless in the sky near the Big Dipper. I decided that I must be suffering from a slight concussion from when I hit my head on that rock.

Now what was I doing before I fell? Was I coming from somewhere or was I going to somewhere? That's funny, I can't seem to remember. If I was going to somewhere, was I going home? I was going home to . . . wait a minute. Where is my home if I was going home? I can't remember where my home is, or if I have one. Okay, now I'm getting scared. If I can't remember where my home is, what is my name? Oh, my gosh! I can't remember what my name is either. I must have what is called amnesia. I heard tell about it being partial or total loss of memory caused by brain injury due to a concussion, shock or trauma. How hard did I hit my head on that damn rock? Am I going to be this way for the rest of my life or is this just temporary?

Okay, I've got to stop scaring myself and be brave. Being brave means being real scared but doing the thing anyway just to get the job done. The first thing I need to do is get a drink of that ice cold water then get over to that dead horse. I crawled over to the water's edge and looked over the bank. The water was so clear I could see clean down to the bottom. I took off my neckerchief and wet it down then put the cold cloth to the bump and the gash on my head, holding it there to reduce the swelling. Of course there was pain the instant I did that. I struggled over to the dead horse, shooed away the vultures, and took the canteen off the saddle. I struggled back to the river and filled it with clean cold water from the river, took a good drink and capped it, then looped it over my head. Just in case I passed out again I would always have fresh water hanging on me when I woke up.

I crawled back over to the dead horse, and it was a battle to remove the heavy saddle with the weight of the horse laying on the tight cinches. I noticed the horse's hind quarters had the markings of what looked like a Flying T2 Brand on it. I did not recollect that brand. The horse was a good-looking roan-colored quarter horse. It couldn't be more than five years old. If it was my horse it surely was a very big loss. I looked back up the mountain to the trail above and no way in hell could man or beast survive a fall from that trail from as far up as it appeared to be. It was a gift that the ledge caught me and I survived. It would have been an even bigger God given gift if I hadn't hit my head and lost my memory. Guess I can't expect to be lucky all the time! I unhitched the saddle and struggled to pull it from the horse, dragging it by the saddle horn off the trail's edge into a clearing in a nearby wooded area. That little clearing was a life-saving distance away from the stink of the dead horse and the gluttonous vultures. I stopped to catch my breath.

I pulled the bedroll from under the cantle and made myself a nice soft place to lay down and go to sleep when the falling darkness would arrive. Then I gathered some kindling and made a campfire. That too, was an effort for me to do. A five pound bag of coffee beans was in the saddle bags along with a coffee pot and a coffee cup. I made a pot of coffee. Suddenly I remembered to check that my gun had a full round in it, then pulled the rifle from its scabbard and filled it full of rounds, also. This prepared me for any kind of surprise attack from anything Mother Nature decided to throw at me. There was enough jerky left in the grub sack for my supper and I ate it all.

I turned the saddle upside down on the bedroll to make a pillow for my head and that's when I saw it. On the underside of the saddle, printed in capital letters, was the name SUNDELL. Now was that the name of the one who owned the saddle or was that the horse's name? The name didn't ring a bell and no way in hell could I remember a thing or recognize the name on the saddle or the brand on the horse. My next question, was Sundell a first name or a last name? This was a pretty scary situation. I sat down on my bedding and started going through all my pockets. Maybe something on me would give me some clue as to my identification. If not, from now on my name will be Sundell should anyone ask and the saddle is now mine.

In the back pocket of my jeans was a penknife and a bandanna much smaller in size than the neckerchief I had around my neck. Burned into the wooden knife handle was the name Sundell, printed by the same hand that wrote it onto the saddle. Well that clinched it; I was definitely Sundell because this knife in my pocket belongs to me. Not only that, I was sure I was a cowboy. My saddle was packed heavy for herding cows and roping horses. A small packet of Bull Durum chew, what was left of it, was in my left front jeans pocket. In my left front shirt pocket was a slip of paper that scared the hell out of me. It was a note to me.

TO SUNDELL,

RECEIVED FOUR ROUGH STOCK STALLIONS IN FULFILLMENT OF T2 CONTRACT. PAID HIM TWO THOUSAND DOLLARS.

MIKE HAMMER

Well shit and holy hell! I'm supposed to have two thousand dollars on me, and gol-dang it, I don't. I've got to go through all my stuff again and see if I can find that money. I rifled through everything I owned and found nothing. I went back to the dead horse and looked under it and around it and came up with nothing again. A buzzard flew down to peck at me and I drew my pistol lighting fast, and shot it dead center. I just learned something else about myself. I'm one hell of a fast draw and a deadly accurate shot. This information was definitely to my advantage to know from a standpoint of self-defense. Am I a gun slinger or bounty hunter? I wonder?

Going back to the river bank I looked back up at the ledge and could see on top of the ledge I was lying on and nothing but rocks on that ledge; nothing that looked like money, or paper or anything leather like a money belt that may have fallen off of me. Thank God because no way in hell could I climb back up there to retrieve anything I may have dropped on that ledge. Now how did I lose that money and where did I lose it! Who was this Mike Hammer? Was the Flying T2 Brand the spread or the brand I worked for and belonged to? I must work for the brand since the brand was on my horse. Even worse yet, was the money stolen off me while I was out cold or did I drop it in the ravine as my horse fell? This whole situation was a mystery.

A cold chill in the air reminded me that darkness was falling fast and I needed to lay down and get some rest at my campsite. I was feeling exhausted, confused and weak. More than anything I needed the sleep and I could look for the money in the morning. My biggest problem was how do I get back up to the top of that mountain trail to even look for it? I have no horse. Would I have to walk back up from this lower part of the trail following it uphill to the top rim from where I fell? It would take me hours to walk back up there and look for the money I may have dropped when my horse lost its footing and fell over the edge. Back at my campsite, I poured myself another cup of hot black coffee, drank it down, settled my guns around me, put my head back and tried to rest.

~~~ T2 Brand ~~~

Just prior to Sundell's climbing down off that ledge, Westley Payson was on his way to Brotherhood, California to meet up with the rest of the outlaw gang Dash Cogburn was running. It was in their plans to all meet in town so they could rob the local bank. He took the shortcut off the Bitter End Trail that was just a soft sandy path running through the woods and winding down the mountain's slope. Halfway down the mountain, where the trail leveled off near a clearing, there was a stream called Musky River, where the outlaw gang usually watered their horses and stopped to rest. The first thing Payson noticed was the buzzards attracting his attention to a dead horse down in the ravine. He decided to dismount and while his horse drank water he would climb down there to check it out and maybe look for a dead body. As near as he could figure someone's horse slipped off the soft shoulder of the upper trail and met its death in the ravine.

When he finally reached the horse, he looked around for its rider and could find nothing or no one in the area. He decided to check in the saddle bags for any information he could find on who owned the animal or where it came from, since he did not recognize the brand on the horse. To his great surprise there was a stash of cash in one of the pockets of the saddle bags. *Wow*, he thought. If the owner is dead, the cash is mine. He took his time counting it and found out it was two thousand dollars. He climbed out of the ravine and back up to the trail, took the reins of his horse and walked it into the clearing. Westley decided to hide the money and return for it at a later date when he was alone and away from the rest of the gang. He stashed it in the hollow of a tree he found just inside the clearing. None of the other gang members had to know about this. It was his secret alone. He grabbed the saddle horn and hauled himself up onto his horse and continued on down the trail to meet up with the other gang members in Brotherhood, California.

CHAPTER II

BROTHERHOOD, CALIFORNIA

The town of Brotherhood, California was thirty miles northwest of the small town of Brawley, California, the town where the Flying T2 Ranch did a lot of stock business with the local ranchers. Brotherhood had a much larger population than the small border town of Brawley. The Wright Brother's General Store boasted in newspaper ads that it had an "endless variety" of merchandise to offer and it was all under one roof. They even boasted they had a Montgomery Ward & Co. catalogue you could order from at wholesale prices right from the grange supply house in Chicago, Illinois. This boasting brought a lot of retail business into the store making the Wright Brother's rich by the standards of their time. The Wright Brothers kept all their riches in the Brotherhood National Bank.

Next door to the General Store was Denver Freighting Company owned by a father and daughter team, Robert and Rosey Denver. They were not a well to do company but they managed to get by just making ends meet from month to month. Next door to the freight company was the Brotherhood Hash House. A small sign on the front post boasted, "Anything you don't eat goes to the cat and the dog!"

The first door east of the Brotherhood Hash House was Dave's Barber Shop. The front window announced shaving, shampooing and haircutting done in the latest fashion. Next to that was the Stockman's Saloon and a sign on the wall by the batwing doors said "wines, liquors, & cigars, also a billiard table".

There was a fire arms and ammunition store called "Brotherhood Guns and Ammo", Proprietor: Walter Sevensky. It also sold lumber and stoves, agricultural implements and would repair guns and pistols while you wait. A store titled "Boot and Shoe Makers", Proprietor Bart Mullen, bragged a good fit guaranteed and the best of materials used. At the end of the street was "Brotherhood Livery", Feed and Stables, James Bell, Proprietor.

The first building across the street was a watchmaker and dealer in rings, jewelry, and diamonds. Sheriff John Bridges had his office next door to the watchmaker's repair shop. There were a couple more saloons with dance halls on that same side of the street and the Brotherhood National Bank was next to a ladies dress shop.

There was a city ordinance that stated it was unlawful for any person to ride a horse or mule at a faster gait than six miles per hour within the city limits. However, that ordnance was not obeyed on this day by five gunman who entered into town with plans to rob the bank. Rob it they did and left at a much faster gait than six miles per hour. It was bad enough that they robbed the bank but they broke an ordnance as they did it! Sheriff John Bridges was furious! He needed to form a posse and go after those outlaws and run them down. There was no way they would get away with robbing the bank *and* breaking an ordinance in *his* town.

The problem was much bigger than the sheriff imagined though. He was stunned when he later found out Rosey Denver was in the bank making a deposit when the outlaws burst in to do the robbery. Rosey, the buckskin clad freight wagon driver and clerk, was a witness to the whole thing. So rather than shoot and kill the good looking young woman, the outlaws kidnapped her, taking her with them as a hostage. The towns' folk were horrified about what the outlaws would do to the young woman, after all they did shoot and kill the manager and two bank tellers. Would the girl be violated, mistreated or what, questioned the town folks. After all, she was only fifteen or sixteen years old.

Sheriff Bridges formed a posse and they trailed the outlaws for a couple days and lost the trail in the mountains high up near the Bitter End Trail. They returned to Brotherhood disappointed that they were not successful. Next day Bob Denver took the freight wagon alone on a run to Brawley, California, since Rosey was no longer there to do the job with him. He notified the sheriff in Brawley about the robbery and his missing daughter. The sheriff searched the town of Brawley but did not find any clues in his town as to what may have happened to Rosey Denver. She was certainly not in the town of Brawley. Bob Denver returned to Brotherhood with a very broken heart. At least Sheriff Bridges and Deputy Jim Cole of Brotherhood telegraphed several nearby towns to be on the lookout for the outlaws and the missing girl.

<p style="text-align:center">~~~ T2 Brand ~~~</p>

Dash Cogburn was an outlaw and gunman. He was the leader of a band of out of work cowboys who were down on their luck. They took up with Dash for a means to gain some fast spending money, liquor and good times. After a few robberies, and some cattle rustling that went very well, the bunch of down and out cowhands stayed with him and had no trouble taking his orders. Dash had a rude personality and was rugged and unkempt in his appearance. He did some time in Yuma prison, and by the way his life was now going, it wouldn't be long before he would make a visit back to Yuma prison permanently.

J. W. Powell was a good looking, clean shaven, young cowboy who stayed on with the bunch because he did not have to work so hard for the easy money and the women. The gang called him JW. Greg Wills was friends with JW when they joined the gang. Anything JW did Greg followed along in his footsteps like a shadow and blood brother.

Westley Payson was a drinker, a gambler and card shark. He was not afraid to use his gun against anyone he thought was a threat to him. Like Dash, he possessed an ornery, cantankerous, and independent personality.

When this band of outlaws left Brotherhood, California with the bank money, they decided to take a shortcut on the soft mountain trail across the craggy mountain passes to the plains, and on to the mining town of Chloride, where they had a hideout in the mountains above Chloride. This rugged, dangerous cattle trail cut off from the Bitter End Trail northeast across the mountains way above Yuma, and was a shortcut to the mining town. Very few riders took this trail because it was treacherous with jagged cut rocks and very narrow with sand in spots that could give way and cause a horse and rider to fall down off the mountain trail into deep ravines and rock crevices. This band of outlaws used this trail often and knew where the bad spots were and their horses were as sure-footed as mountain goats having trekked many times in single file on this steep, sandy trail. They travelled for a couple hours, heading uphill on the trail, until they came to Musky River where they knew they could water their horses and rest in a clearing not so far off the deserted trail.

"Hey, Dash. That's the dead horse I told you about that I found on the way down this trail yesterday when I was to meet you in town. Except yesterday he had a saddle on him," said Wesley.

"Looks like the vultures had a feast. Boy does he stink. If he had a saddle on him what happened to it?"

"I don't know, Dash. Someone must have helped themselves to the saddle. I checked through the belongings and there was nothing much but an almost empty grub sack. Even the grub sack is gone. I left the saddle on the horse after looking around for a dead body. There was none so I left, not to waste any time getting into Brotherhood to meet the rest of you for the bank job," replied Wesley.

"Why would anyone steal the saddle? This trail is less travelled than the Bitter End Trail. It is seldom that anyone has reason to travel through here. That's why we use it so much. It's off the beaten path. Maybe someone was lost or was using it as a shortcut to the Bitter End Trail from the ranch lands outside of Brotherhood and Brawley."

"You never know, Dash. Evidently, someone was using it and their horse lost its footing on a sandy spot on the upper part of the trail. How else would a horse wind up dead in the ravine?"

"Let's check our canteens, fill them with water and use that clearing off the trail to rest our horses," replied Dash. "JW ride our back trail and check and make sure no one is following us, especially the posse. Greg, get the girl down off her horse and give her some water. Watch her and make sure she don't try to run away. If she runs, shoot her!"

The gang dismounted walking their horses to the familiar clearing where they usually rested while travelling that nameless mountain trail that forked off from the infamous Bitter End Trail. To the shock and surprise of the outlaws, there sleeping on a bedroll with his head and shoulders resting on the underside of his saddle was a young cowboy. He had a bruised up appearance like he had been badly hurt.

Even though he was eighteen years old his good looks made him look more like sixteen and younger than he actually was. The sounds of the horses and the talking of the outlaws aroused the sleeping cowboy, and he did a lighting fast draw the same time as Dash drew in surprise, neither of them firing their side arms. It was very obvious to Dash as well as the others that the young cowboy was lightning fast and outdrew Dash by a mile. In a nervous tone Dash asked, "Who, uh, who the hell are you, mister?"

"I'm called Sundell," said the cowboy. Sundell slowly holstered his gun.

"Sundell, what?" asked Dash, as he also slowly holstered his gun.

"Just Sundell, nothing else," replied the cowboy.

"Where the hell did you come from?" asked Dash.

"I fell from that upper trail on the top of this mountain," replied Sundell pointing his finger straight up.

"You fell from that trail up there and lived? You got one gol-dang hard head if you did. (Laughter from the gang.) Is that your horse we just passed in the ravine by the river?"

"Sure is. I'm awful hungry. Ain't ate nothin' since yesterday. My supplies are all gone. You got anything I can eat?"

"What do we got in our saddle bags, boys? Give this man something to eat. Anybody that can fall off the mountain from that trail up above, and live, must be wearing a set of angel wings," said Dash. (More laughter from the gang.)

"Here Dash. I've some jerky he can have," said Greg Wills.

"Terry. Build up this guy's campfire some more. Rosey. Get your ass over here and put a pot of coffee on for the boys."

Just then JW rode in and quickly dismounted. "Trail's clear, Dash. Everything's okay. Nobody is following. Who's this guy?"

"That's what I'm trying to find out. Says his name is Sundell, nothing else. Seems to me he dropped down from heaven. (Laughter from the gang.) Where you from cowboy?"

"Don't rightly know," replied Sundell.

"What do you mean, you don't know? You were born, am I right?" said Dash. "So where were you born?"

"Don't rightly know that," replied Sundell, again.

"Hey, Dash. Maybe he was hatched?" kidded Wesley. (Laughter from the gang.)

Dash turned and looked at the boys and laughed. He turned back looking at the cowboy.

"So how old are you? Do you know how old you are?"

"Don't know, mister. Pert near close to nineteen, I guess. I'm still young," said Sundell.

"Why you don't look much older than sixteen boy. How come you can't answer any of my questions? What's the matter with you?" said Dash. "Are you dumb?"

"Well, it was like this. When my horse lost its footing on the sandy edge of the upper trail and fell off the mountain, it hit that ledge on the way down, throwing me off onto that flat area up there, which is jutting out of the mountainside. I hit my head on a rock and I don't know how long I was out cold. My horse didn't survive the fall. When I woke up there was blood on the rock where my head hit and split open, I couldn't climb up so I climbed down the rocks to get to my saddle and canteen. I pulled my saddle off my horse and dragged it into this here clearing. I hurt my head bad when it hit the rocks on that ledge and I think I have what they call amnesia. I'm not sure though. The only thing I know is my name; can't remember anything about my past. I've got one gosh-awful bad headache."

Dash figured whoever this cowboy was he was a loner, a super-fast draw with that gun of his and most likely just as accurate a shot. By the way his saddle was packed he must have been working cattle. He had a careful silence about him that made Dash curious to want to know more about him. He was not telling much about his background either. Could it be he was running from the law?

"That's some story, fella. You don't have a horse and you don't have a home that you know of to go to, so maybe you better join up with us. I can use a real fast gun like yours. It wouldn't make any sense to leave a fast gun like you to die on the trail. We are heading back to our cabin in the mountains. It's a good size cabin kind of like a bunkhouse. We live there when we are not working. We can leave you here to rot without food or transportation or you can join up with us. What do you say kid?" said Dash.

"You're right. I can't stay here alone. I'm hurt and I need food and help. Take me with you."

"All right. Come with us then. They call me Dash. I'm boss of this group of boys." Dash offered his hand for a shake. Sundell shook hands with him. "Hey, bitch. Is that coffee ready yet. Pour Sundell a cup. Soon as the horses are rested up we're leaving again. JW he can ride double with you," said Dash.

Sundell didn't exactly like the tone with which Dash treated the girl that was with them and he frowned. Rosey poured a cup of coffee for Sundell and held it while he took sips of it. "Sip it slow, mister. You look badly bruised. I'll clean up those bloody scrapes and that gash on your head when we get to wherever it is we are going." Sundell looked up into the girl's face and decided she was a pretty little thing. *If she wants to patch me up, hell yes, its fine with me and anything else she wants to do for me,* he thought.

"How are you involved with these boys, miss? You a part of this bunch?" inquired Sundell.

"No, sir, cowboy. I'm their captive. They robbed the national bank in Brotherhood and kidnapped me because I was in the bank at the time, and I'm a witness. They killed three people."

"Shut up, you," yelled Dash. "Keep your mouth shut, Rosey, or I'll shut it for you."

Rosey handed the cup of coffee to Sundell, cowering away to a spot by herself. Sundell was now beginning to understand the picture here. Rosey was a prisoner and was being mistreated. This was a gang of outlaws probably running from the law. He had no choice but to stick with them until he could get out of a very bad situation. It would be to Rosey's benefit if he stuck with the gang to protect her from them. He had to play along with them for Rosey's sake and his own predicament. There was no choice but to play it cautious and become part of the gang. He had no idea who he was, but he did know that he didn't approve of treating a woman the way they were treating Rosey. That's the second thing he learned about himself. First, he was a deadly fast draw and a very accurate shot and second he was raised with morals pummeled into him and he somehow knew that women were treated with respect. The only thing Sundell had doubts about is, was joining this gang to save his own skin and Rosey's, going to be the worst decision he ever made in his lifetime. He was soon to find out.

When the horses were rested, the gang continued along the trail until they came to the trail's end on the other side of the mountain. They took another break to rest their horses before moving on across the plains. JW again scouted the trail ahead of them and on the plains. When JW signaled all was clear they moved on across the plains and up another mountain trail to a cabin hideout in the rugged country above the rough mining town of Chloride.

It was there they unloaded everything and settled into the hideout. A sentry was posted on the trail leading up to the hideout.

"Hey, Rosey. Make us a meal, bitch. You'll find everything you need in that cabinet over there." Dash pointed to a cupboard.

"I'm not making anything for you. Make it yourselves," said Rosey. "You got along fine without me before."

Dash walked up to her and backhanded her across the face. "You'll do as I say and cook us a meal. Just because you wear buckskins like a man and drive a freight wagon doesn't mean you can't do women's work. You'll do your share of the work around here and you'll take orders from me. Understand? Now get busy we're hungry."

"But I was going to patch up Sundell's scrapes and cuts and check the gash on his head. It may need a couple stitches to close it up. He needs to be looked after."

"You'll do as I said." Dash grabbed her arm and shoved her towards the cabinet causing her to stumble almost falling on the hard wood floor.

"I'm okay, Rosey. Do as he says," said Sundell. "C'mon Dash. Take it easy on her. She's a girl. You're libel to hurt her."

"What's this? The battered up cowboy suddenly grows a set balls when it comes to wimmen folk?" (Laughter sounded from the gang.)

"It's nothing like you think, Dash. I just don't cotton to hurting ladies."

"Hey boys. We got a new gentleman in our group! He thinks Rosey is a lady! Looks to me like the cowboy got an interest in this here muleskinning, britches-wearing, freight-wagon-driving, and boyish-girl. Ha, ha."

"Take it easy, Dash. I just have respect for girls is all," said Sundell. "You might get a little more co-operation out of her if you show her some respect and dispense with the name calling."

"Oh yeah. Well I'll lay off her and ease up on her when you claim her. Until then it's like I just said. Make us a meal, bitch! Sundell looks like he's a tough enough cowboy. His injuries will keep until after dinner. Now get started on that meal," ordered Dash.

Rosey found the fixings and prepared a large pot of beef stew with vegetables. They all ate in shifts. Sundell, Rosey and the sentry, who just switched guard with another man, ate last. Sundell noticed that Rosey did a good job on the stew. For what she had to work with, she was a damn good cook. He chowed down and took a second helping. It was quite a while since he ate a good meal. After she cleaned up the supper dishes, Rosey found a bottle of ninety proof whiskey and used it to clean dirt out of the scrapes and cuts on various parts Sundell's body. He winced and inhaled a deep breath from the pain but did not let out a sound.

"I'm sorry. I don't mean to hurt you," whispered Rosey. "If I don't clean out these scrapes they will get infected."

"Yes, ma'am," replied Sundell. "Much obliged for your help."

Then Rosey took a needle and piece of thread and put four stitches in the open cut on Sundell's head. Wow did that hurt. His eyes teared from the pain.

Dash looked over at him and laughed at the facial expressions, but was impressed that no sounds came out of Sundell. "See! I told you he was tough. Anybody that can fall off that mountain trail and live to tell about it, is nothing but tough! He should be a good asset to this gang."

"I hope you're right boss," said JW. "We lost Bart in that last raid."

"Ain't nothing I can do about Bart. He was too slow getting out of the way. All right boys. Let's get some rest. We can all use some shut-eye. There's only four bunks in this shack. Anybody without a bunk just throw your bedroll on the floor. That includes Sundell and the girl. Terry. Bank the fire for the night."

Sundell waited until Terry banked the fire then threw down his own bedroll. Taking Rosey's bedroll he placed it next to his own bedroll, keeping himself between the other men and Rosey. It was a protective instinct he was sensing but never knew why. No one seemed to notice what he did, not even Rosey.

~~~ T2 Brand ~~~

Late in the night Sundell woke up to a soft whimpering sound near him. It was Rosey, and her teeth were chattering. She was cold and crying. He looked over at her and she was not sleeping. The temperature in the mountains had dropped considerably over night and Rosey could not get warm. The large log on the banked fire was ebbing very low and slow, not giving off as much heat from the fireplace as was needed to warm the building.

"Excuse me, ma'am," he whispered to Rosey. "You're freezing and if you don't get warmed up you'll catch your death of cold. I can make you only one offer, and I don't mean it to sound like I'm being fresh. You can roll over here under my blanket with me and put your blanket over the top of us both. That way we will both have two blankets on us."

"Are you crazy?" she whispered back. "Not on your best day, cowboy, would I fall for that!"

"Please, ma'am. I'm only trying to help you. You can trust me. Honest. I'm offering you a choice. It's up to you what you want to do." Sundell rolled over to try and go back to sleep. Rosey shivered for a while longer, then changed her mind.

"Hey Sundell," she whispered.

"Yes ma'am?"

"Okay cowboy. I'll take you up on your offer, but you make one false move and you'll suffer my wrath."

"Yes, ma'am," said Sundell smiling. "I certainly don't want to suffer your wrath!" He lifted up one side of his wool blanket and Rosey scooted under it lying next to him. Together they fixed her blanket over the top of them both. Sundell rolled on his side putting his back to her. Rosey snuggled up against him. He found that he couldn't go to sleep. "Hey! Stop that," he turned and whispered to her.

"Stop what?" whispered Rosey in return.

"Stop wiggling around like that against my backside. You're arousing me, ma'am. I ain't gonna apologize for being a man if a surprise something happens by accident."

"Oh! I'm sorry. I didn't realize it," said Rosey. "I'm not used to being this close to a man. Actually, I never slept with one before." *I needed to know that*, thought Sundell.

"Just lay very still and go to sleep, ma'am. Don't go wiggling all around. My body heat will warm you soon enough."

"Okay," said Rosey. She smiled to herself. *I'm not accustomed to sleeping with a man*, she thought. *I was just trying to find a comfortable position. Never realized what it was doing to him. Guess I've got some learning to do about men. She silently smiled again. No way in hell do I want to arouse him and cause a problem. It was never my intention.* She fell asleep and slept peacefully and warm until morning.

~~~ T2 Brand ~~~

When morning arrived the sun's light intruded into the cabin at a very fast pace. Terry was up first and he looked around for Rosey to get her prepping their breakfast. He did not see her right away and then he saw her movement under Sundell's blankets. That's when he realized she was *sleeping* with Sundell.

He hurried over to Dash to wake him up. "Hey, Dash. Come here and get a look at this will ya. Rosey's sleeping with Sundell."

"She's what?" said Dash.

"Come here. Lookie here." Terry pointed to the two bodies wrapped up together in the blankets on the floor. Rosey was wrapped up tight in Sundell's arms as they slept entwined together on the floor. Sometime during the night, Sundell unconsciously rolled over and wrapped himself around her in his sleep.

Dash walked over to the two of them and stood over them with his hands fixed on both hips. He toed Sundell with his boot to wake him up with a startle.

"Sundell. Just what the *hell* do you think you're doing with the freight-wagon bitch? You got an explanation for this? I'm waiting for an answer," scolded Dash.

Sundell woke up stunned. Rubbing the sleep from his eyes he was trying to come awake. Unwinding from the girl he stretched his arms and shoulders looking up at Dash and Terry.

"What?" he said sleepily. "What's the matter?"

"What do you think you are doing sleeping all wrapped around the freight-wagon bitch?"

"She woke up cold and shivering during the night, Dash," he said. "I offered her my blanket and body heat to help keep her warm. That's all," explained Sundell.

"By the looks of the two of you, there's no doubt in my mind how you used your body heat last night to warm the bitch up. You claiming her, Sundell?"

One at a time the other gang members were slowly getting up to see what the shouting was all about. The noise aroused Rosey, also.

"C'mon, Dash. Lighten up. Will you," said Sundell throwing the covers off. "We still got our clothes on." Sundell forgot he was used to sleeping with the fly of his pants unbuttoned for a loose comfortable feeling while he slept in his tight jeans.

"Looks to me like he already claimed her during the night Dash," belted out Payson, as he stared at the open fly on Sundell's pants, and the very large bulge of Sundell's well-endowed manhood. It was trying to peek out of his red long johns as it protruded out of the open fly of his jeans.

"Shut up Payson. Let me handle this. Well, I'm waiting. You claiming her or not. You claim her and she's your responsibility."

Sundell suddenly realized what Dash was suggesting and thought about it for a minute and then made a quick decision. He had no choice but to keep these ornery animals away from the young girl. Especially knowing what he now knew.

"Yeah. I'm claiming her, Dash. The girl belongs to me and nobody better get any ideas about abusing her or they'll have my gun to answer to," said Sundell.

"All right, boys. You heard him. He's claiming the bitch and she's his responsibility alone. Nobody lays a hand on the girl without Sundell's permission. Everybody understand that?"

"Aw boss that ain't fair," wined Westley Payson. "Why does he get the girl? She should go to a regular gang member, one who's been around for a long time."

"You heard me. The girl is Sundell's. It's pretty evident he already claimed her last night. Stay away from her. That goes for all of you."

No more questions were asked. Sundell wasn't sure why he did it but he knew he was in for a lot of responsibility with this girl. She would probably cause him a lot of trouble. However, she was better off with him than with any of the others. He guessed the girl was a virgin when she hinted to him during the night that she'd never before slept with a man. Whether the girl knew it or not, he was experienced when it came to sleeping with women, so he wasn't exactly her savior. He would try like hell to behave himself since she seemed to be much younger than himself.

~~~ T2 Brand ~~~

Rosey rolled out from under the blankets and got up to start the breakfast. That is when she noticed Sundell's open fly and the very large bulge. She quickly looked the other way so as not to stare at him there. Sundell got up also and folded both blankets and set them on the floor in the corner.

Realizing his fly was unbuttoned and loose, he quickly turned his back to the girl and buttoned it close. Now he realized why everyone was so riled. This looked very bad on his part. *Oh well*, he thought. *They will have to get over it. Maybe it would work out for the better. They could think what they wanted. I'll just keep the charade going.* He walked over to the window and looked out. It was rather breezy in the mountains.

"Hey Dash. I'm gonna need a horse since I lost mine. You got any suggestions? I can't keep riding double."

"Yeah. There's a canyon about three miles out on the other side of the hill from this cabin. You can rope a wild horse over there. But you'll have to train him by yourself to take a rider. None of us can do it for you. We ain't horse wranglers."

"Thanks. I can do it. I'd like to borrow your horse after breakfast and some rope. If it's okay with you."

"I'm not going anywhere. I've got to split up our shares of this bank money. You understand that you don't get any this time around. You weren't in on this bank robbery. You'll get a share next time."

"I knew that, Dash. I got my own little problem that has to get solved. I lost some money when I fell off that sandy, narrow trail. I've got to go back and look for it in the ravine."

"What do you mean you lost money?" said Dash.

"Well it was probably in my saddle bags. That is where I would've put it. My saddle bags were empty when I got back to my horse and saddle and checked through everything. I even looked under my dead horse."

Dash was suddenly thinking very hard. *Did Westley lie to me when he said he checked the saddle bags on the dead horse and nothing much was in them? There was no dead body around because the body was out cold on the ledge above. Something about Westley's story is beginning to sound funny to me. It isn't matching up with Sundell's story. I wonder exactly how much money it was that Sundell lost? He is not saying. No reason for him to go back and search the ravine if it was just a few bucks. It must have been something significant. If it was a significant amount, and Westley took it from the saddle bags and didn't share it with the rest of us, he is in for some damn big trouble from me.* Dash temporarily kept his suspicions to himself.

"Breakfast is ready," said Rosey as she set the plates on the table. Everyone gathered around to fill their plates as Rosey poured the coffee, filling up each cup.

"Thank you, Rosey," said Sundell, as she filled his coffee cup.

"Lookie here," said Westley. "The fast gunman with the big balls and the hot body got manners, too."

"You could use a few lessons in manners, Payson," said Sundell.

"I got no use for manners," growled Payson. "Manners are for wimps like you, Sundell."

"Don't call me a wimp you scum. I'm convinced you were raised in a cesspool."

Payson stood up from the table and drew his gun, but Sundell's draw was faster since he saw it coming and was ready for it. Dash stood up and yelled, stop it, at them both before any shots were fired.

"I ain't takin' that insult from him Dash. I mean to do something about it," said Payson.

"Then take your argument outside. The two of you should have it out. No gunplay in here you squash heads. Take your fight outside and settle it a man's way with fists. Now both of you put up the guns and finish it outside. I can't afford to lose any men to gunplay among ourselves. Now both of you spoiled children get the hell outside and get it over with. Settle it up."

They did not hesitate removing their guns and holsters. The boys were ready to scrap. The rest of the gang were already placing bets as to the winner.

Rosey felt shaky and scared. She didn't want anything to happen to Sundell. He was her protection from the others even though he was the newest member of this gang. Sundell was the only one that was kind to her. Rosey already stitched him up once. She feared if anything happened to him, her very safety and security would be compromised. She was in a very bad situation here. When Sundell unbuckled his gun belt he handed it to Rosey to hold. She felt honored to be trusted by him. Payson threw his gun belt on his bunk. The two men walked outside to confront each other as their excitement built up. The others followed to see the show.

"No rules," Dash yelled out. "Get as dirty as you want."

Sundell drew a straight line in the sand. They both positioned on each side of the line, keeping the line between them as they began to circle around it. Payson tried to kick Sundell in the crotch and fight dirty. Sundell jumped back and Payson missed him. Shouts erupted from the on-lookers. The two men continued to circle, then Sundell stepped in hitting Payson hard with a right fist to the jaw. He ducked a right swing from Payson and connected to Payson's jaw with a left hook. Payson went down on the ground. Sundell waited for Payson to get up, but when he did, Payson dove on top of Sundell knocking him into the dirt. They rolled in the dirt lashing out at each other, then got up again. Payson wedged Sundell against the well housing and tried choking him. Sundell's face was turning red from loss of air but his strength won out over Payson's strength and he broke free. Payson pulled a knife from his boot and threw it. Sundell ducked and the knife lodged in the well's side beam next to his head. Sundell gave Payson a fast right hook and then a fast left hook. Payson went down kicking in the dirt. He struggled on the ground for a bit and then went out cold.

"Wow, kid! Where did you learn to fight like that?" complimented Dash.

"I don't know," replied Sundell. "It just seemed to come from out of nowhere." He took the dipper from the bucket wetting down his head and taking a drink. Then he threw the bucket of water on Payson to wake him up. Dash laughed.

"Get up, Payson!" yelled Dash. "Dry off and clean yourself up. You lost that battle! Now make up and be friends with Sundell."

"I don't need him to be friends with me, Dash. With friends like him, I don't need enemies," said Sundell.

Payson got up slowly up on his feet and pointed his finger at Sundell. "I'll get you next time you son-of-a-bitch! This ain't over yet!"

"No it ain't over but I wouldn't try it again you scum-bag. I'm younger and faster than you are." Rosey handed Sundell his holster and he put it back on tying it down at his thigh. She was relieved Sundell won the fight. He was a good fist fighter as well as a fast gun. She could not have asked for a better man to protect her. She was beginning to feel attached to him.

"Come in the cabin and I'll patch up those scrapes and bruises," she said.

"No thanks, ma'am. Much obliged, but I'm fine," replied Sundell.

"But you are bleeding!" said Rosey.

"Thank you, ma'am, but I'm fine."

"Sundell's got vinegar all right," said JW.

Even though he was bleeding, he turned away and walked over to the corral and saddled Dash's horse. He picked up a couple ropes that were hanging from the fence and was more than happy to leave the area and head out to get away from the gang for the day and to try roping a horse of his own.

<center>~~~ T2 Brand ~~~</center>

Rosey was a bit nervous being left alone at the cabin with the rest of the boys. She quickly went inside to start preparing a meal with the hopes they would leave her alone while Sundell was gone. She fully realized Sundell needed to be left alone with his thoughts so he could gather up his wits again. She knew it the minute he turned his back on her and walked away to the corral without saying anything. It was important for him to have that solitude. She needed to give him that private time and protect herself while he was gone. Rosey was beginning to like this cowboy and have romantic feelings for him. She figured out that Sundell was strictly a loner compared to the rest of the gang and that it would be very hard to get close to him and once close to him, it would be even harder to hold on to him. Rosey decided to take her chances with him and take her time with him until she won his trust. He was already showing respect towards her. She felt that was a good beginning for this tough, ornery character. If she could get him to warm up to her, he would protect her with his life from the rest of the outlaw gang. Sundell was her best chance to escape these outlaws. He did not rob the bank or kidnap her and she could see some good in him. Only time would tell if her character assessment of him was correct.

CHAPTER III

A STALLION FOR SUNDELL

There was a bit of a wind kicking up in the air but the weather was clear and dry. Sundell headed out in the direction Dash told him to go. About an hour and a half into his ride he came across a deserted canyon. A stream ran past it and the grass was green and tall for a grazing herd of horses. Sundell noticed a band of horses grazing farther downstream from the canyon. It was a group of mares with juveniles and a dominant stallion. Boy was that black stallion a beauty. The stallion picked his head up and the herd suddenly took off. *I'll have to remember to be quieter*, he thought.

They seemed to like that spot in the stream, thought Sundell. *I've got to figure out a capture sight close to that area. It should be somewhere they would naturally want to go so they travel there on their own while I'm chasing them.*

He scouted around and found a small clearing surrounded by large rocks and trees not too far from the water's edge nearby where the herd was grazing. *I'll make a gate across the front of this clearing using natural materials so it will not harm the horses*, he thought.

Sundell figured that dominant stallion to be about six years of age or older. The foals he sired were about a year or two years old. There were several mares with the band and Sundell figured this stallion was having himself a good old time. *I hate to ruin your fun old boy, but I want you*, he thought. He figured the bay was the dominant mare because she seemed to lead the group to the water and the mineral lick. Her job would also be to guide them to the sheltered places out of the wind in the winter months. This was the mare he needed to trap if he wanted to get that stallion. He hid in the brushwood and watched the movement of the herd for a long time studying their patterns and memorizing their favorite spots to water and graze. The black stallion usually ran at the rear of the herd keeping the slower horses moving and protecting the group from attack of any kind. He watched as the stallion discouraged a young male, who was coming of age, from consorting with the band. *What a smart horse*, he thought. *I want that horse.*

Young females are usually driven off by their mothers if they don't chose to leave the herd when they come into estrous. A young stallion selected a young mare to breed with and guard. This is how wild horses avoid inbreeding. Sundell knew he had to have that black stallion. He would do anything to capture him and train him. That animal was a fast runner. "I'll call him Shadow", he decided.

Sundell made himself a dry camp hidden in the bushes. Then he fashioned a gate across the sheltered clearing he found. *I can chase the band into that clearing and close the gate. Then I can get either the stallion or its dominant mare.*

He waited a couple of hours until the band arrived again at the watering place to drink. *That black stallion senses something wrong*, thought Sundell. *He keeps sniffing the air and pawing the ground. I wonder if he picked up on my scent. I better move out quickly if I want to get him.*

Sundell did a flying mount and took off after the herd, chasing them towards the natural corral. They ran right into the clearing where he wanted them. He closed the gate quickly and to his great surprise the black stallion jumped the gate and took off lightning fast. *Dammit, I missed him! Ghee is he fast. Well, I got the mare. I'll take her back to the cabin and train her to take a rider. I can use her as my second horse and come back for the stallion,* he decided. He roped the mare and tied her to the gate since the darkness was falling at day's end. Then he opened the gate letting the rest of the band go free. It took a couple of hours to tow the bay back to the hideout and put her up in the corral. She showed a lot of resistance. Everyone came running out of the cabin to get a look at the noisy horse.

"Hey Dash! The son-of-a-gun got one. Who would've figured it?"

"Wow! That's a good looking mare, Sundell", said Dash as he ran up to the corral.

"She sure enough is, Dash. You want to see the stallion that got away on me. I'm going back for him this week. He's the one I really want. I can train this mare and keep her as an extra mount."

"If it's that black stallion we been seeing around you'll never catch him, Sundell. He is too fast and rank to tame down. You better be satisfied with this mare."

"I want that horse, Dash, and I intend to catch him."

"You're insane, kid. It will never happen; that horse will kill you first."

"I reckon I'll have to prove you wrong, Dash. Just wait and see. I'll get him because I know just how to do it. That stallion has a fireball of independence built into him! He ran like he was trying to catch the wind!"

"Where did you learn so much about horses? You raised on a ranch or something? I never figured on you catching anything but a snake bite. Ha, ha, ha."

"Don't know, Dash. It must be a gift I guess."

"What are you gonna name the mare, Sundell?" asked Westley.

"Don't know. I thought maybe I'd let Rosey name it. What do you think, Rosey? Give her a name."

"Okay. I like the name Stardust. What do you think, Sundell?"

"Yeah. I like that, too. Good job Rosey. If I catch and train that black stallion I might consider giving Stardust to you. Would you like that?"

"Oh, Sundell, I would love it!"

"Oh, Sundell, I would love it," repeated Dash in a high pitched voice. "Don't even think about taking off or running away on that horse or I'll shoot you deader than a jackrabbit. I wouldn't think twice about it either."

"Take it easy, Dash! Rosey is my responsibility and I'll make sure she don't do that," said Sundell.

"You just make sure you keep an eye on her, cowboy, or I'll have your damn hide, too, and it won't be very pleasant for you."

"I hear you, Dash."

"You hear me, huh? Just see that you remember it, Sundell!"

~~~ *T2 Brand* ~~~

For the next couple of days Sundell gently worked the mare teaching her to take a saddle and bridle. On the third day he was riding in the saddle. The mare gentled and trained very well with this master horseman. Rosey watched every day as Sundell worked with Stardust and on the third day, Stardust surprised everyone. When Sundell came up to the corral leaning on the upper rail, she walked right up to him and nuzzled him. No one could believe it how the mare showed a fondness for her trainer. Sundell was a bit surprised himself as he smiled wide and slightly jerked his head in approval. He handed her a little treat and Stardust accepted it.

"My little girl is a sweetheart," he said. "No wonder that black stallion loved you."

That night in the cabin they were all talking about how well Sundell trained the mare and how good she was reacting when a screaming, stormy horse was making a ruckus out at the corral. Sundell jumped up and was the first one out the door. He knew it was the black stallion looking for its mare. He knew by heart the sound of that scream. No mistaking it. He heard it enough out near the canyon to recognize it. However, he never thought the black devil would wander this close to the cabin to free its mate. He greatly underestimated the power and drive of that horse. Sundell grabbed a rope and tried to lasso it, and it reared at him putting him off balance and knocking him down on the ground. JW came up close to Sundell with a rifle in his hand.

"Stay back, JW! Stay back," screamed Sundell. "Don't shoot him!" JW did as Sundell requested, tossing the rifle to Sundell who caught it in midair from his position on the ground. The black stallion reared again even closer to Sundell and he cranked the rifle firing in the air several times close to the black, from a lying position, scaring the horse who turned and ran like lightning for the hills.

Sundell lay there on the ground panting heavily and swallowing hard trying to catch his breath. Stardust was circling the corral, rearing, and making lots of noise in an effort to break out. JW was the first one to reach Sundell.

"You okay?" he questioned. He helped Sundell up into a sitting position.

"Do I look okay?" replied Sundell. He was as white as a sheet.

"I've seen you look a hell of lot better," answered JW. "That black damn near killed you."

"God, is he a beauty! He was after his mare; was probably watching me work her from up in those hills. Tried to free her. Damn near did it, too. Didn't I tell you he runs like he's chasing the wind?"

"Sundell, are you crazy? Stardust is the black's mare? That horse will kill you for sure for stealing his mare!"

"JW. He can try to kill me but not before I capture him and train him. And I intend to do just that."

"Kid. You are definitely insane. I'm convinced of it now. Your head must have hit that mountain rock pretty damn hard! It scrambled all your brains! That horse will be back to kill us all!"

"Tell you what. I'll go back out after him first thing in the morning. That way he won't come back here. Help me up, JW. I strained some muscles and I'm in pain."

"You fool," said Dash. "That rank horse is mad. Release that mare and let her go. You can always get another one; you seem to be a good wrangler."

"Sorry, Dash. I can't do that. I'm halfway there. I caught Stardust for a reason. She is going to bring him right to me where I can capture him. I won't release her now for any reason. She is my bait for him. He just proved that to me. I mean to train that horse and make him mine. My plan is working. I'm not quitting now."

"You are a nut case, Sundell. I should have left your fucking hide on that trail to die where I found it. Never should have picked you up." Dash walked back to the cabin shaking his head. The rest of the gang followed behind him making bets with each other on the capture of the black stallion. At least it was something amusing to do while waiting to take on another bank job.

JW helped Sundell stand up. Rosey ran up to Sundell as he brushed the dirt off his clothes. He handed the rifle back to JW. "Thanks a lot for the rifle, JW. It saved me a trampling." JW just shook his head.

"Are you okay, Sundell?" said Rosey. "I was so scared he would trample you!"

"I'm fine, Rosey. I'll live to see that horse another day. I aim to catch him and train him."

"Dash is right. You *are* half crazy," said Rosey. She turned and headed back to the cabin. Sundell just laughed as he watched her tramp away.

Sundell and JW walked over to the corral. JW watched as Sundell climbed through the rails and calmed down the mare. *He sure does have a way with horses*, thought JW. *Wonder where all his horse sense came from. He knows a lot more than any of us about livestock.*

"Let's go get some shuteye, JW. I reckon I'll go out early in the morning and look for that horse," said Sundell. They left the corral and headed back to the cabin to turn in for the night.

~~~ *T2 Brand* ~~~

As the men were settling down in their beds for the night, Rosey was finishing up the dishes and straightening up the cooking area. Sundell brazenly walked up to her and grabbed her by the shoulders and kissed her very passionately on the lips. She struggled to break away from him but he was too strong for her. He subdued her and kissed her again. Laughter sounded from the men as they thought Sundell was letting her know who the boss was. *Good it worked* thought Sundell. *I'll just keep the charade going and they won't bother her.*

"Finish up what you are doing and come to bed," ordered Sundell. "I don't intend to wait all night for you. I'm an impatient man." *That ought to impress this gang*, thought Sundell. *Now I got to hope she don't slap me when she comes to bed. If she does, I deserved it!*

Rosey blew out the lamp and settled down into Sundell's bedroll. She was very quiet and didn't talk to him. He giggled to himself. *She's mad all right.* He snuggled up to her back and whispered in her ear.

"Don't be mad Rosey. I just did that for effect. Showing off in front of the boys. I apologize to you for so being fresh."

"I am mad," she whispered back to him. "But I'm also confused. You don't belong in this gang, Sundell."

"Let me be the judge of that, Rosey," he said.

"I think I liked that kiss. Darn you."

"Oh really? How about this then?" He French kissed her on the ear and she pushed him away as he giggled, and at the same time she was quite surprised at how wonderful his tenderness felt. She hated to admit it, but she did actually like it. Although, she didn't want to lead him on. He just might get some more ideas.

"Go to sleep you two," hollered Dash. "You are keeping me awake."

"Sorry, Dash. I'm going to sleep. That near trampling wore me out."

Good. Go to sleep, thought Rosey, *and leave me alone you rascal.*

~~~ *T2 Brand* ~~~

Again, very early in the morning before the others were up, Sundell went out looking to capture that black stallion down at the creek near the canyon. He missed again and again, but never got tired and never gave up on his quest. *I'll try one more time before I go back. It should be dark soon*, he thought. He did try again and had no more luck than before.

~~~ *T2 Brand* ~~~

Meanwhile, Rosey was busy in the kitchen gathering up what she would need to make an evening meal. She was suddenly grabbed from behind in a body lock and someone was fondling her. When she turned her head and looked back it was Payson trying to molest her and have his way with her. She tried to fight him off but he was squeezing her arm so tight she couldn't get free. He turned her towards him and slapped her around for fighting him. He found it amusing that she was fighting hard to resist his advances. This made the game even more fun for him. He was getting quite rough with her bruising her face from slaps and squeezing it with his fist. Rosey screamed in terror and Payson cuffed her so hard with the back of his hand that she fell banging against the table bruising her face close to her eye. Dash and JW came flying in through the door from outside and grabbed him, holding him back from her. JW picked Rosey up off the floor into a standing position. Rosey was trembling and crying.

"What the hell do you think you are doing, Payson!" yelled Dash.

"It ain't fair I tell you. Giving the girl to that brain dead wrangler instead of one of us boys. After all. I'm the one that kidnapped her!"

"She belongs to Sundell. He claimed her. You keep your hands off of her. Now get out of here and go feed the horses. Don't let me catch you bothering her again. Go on, and stay away from her. You hear me?"

Payson left the cabin angry. Dash just shook his head. *This girl is more trouble than she is worth*, thought Dash. JW walked over to Rosey and checked her face.

"He hurt the girl, Dash" said JW. She is gonna have a nasty shiner on that eye. She has bruises and a gash on her face and her arm is black and blue where he squeezed it so hard. No telling what Sundell will do when he gets back and sees this. He ain't gonna like it one bit, Dash. He'll kill Payson for hurting his girl."

"Take care of her, JW. I don't give a shit what Sundell will think or what he will do about Payson. That's his problem. The girl is his responsibility. Payson should never have kidnapped her even though she was a witness to the robbery. Before this is all over, I may have to kill her or force Sundell to do it, and I'm not going to like that at all." He walked out of the cabin heading for the corral. He could care less about the girl.

"I can stop the bleeding on that gash, Rosey, but I can't do anything about the bruises. It will take months for the black and blue to heal," said JW.

"That's okay, JW. I can take care of myself. Thank you for coming in and stopping him."

31

"You're welcome, Miss Rosey. Dash and I were standing next to each other when we heard you scream. I sure as hell don't want to be in Payson's boots when Sundell finds out about this."

"We are not going to tell him, JW. We will keep quiet as much as we can."

"One look at that black eye and he will know, Rosey. He's gonna find out and you can't keep it from him."

"Then we will worry about it when it happens," replied Rosey.

~~~ T2 Brand ~~~

It was early evening when Sundell got back from the canyon without the black stallion again. He checked the mare and worked for a little while with Stardust when he was called to come in for supper. Rosey had cooked venison steaks from the fresh game that Sundell brought in a few nights before. The boys started teasing Sundell about missing the black stallion again. They were all laughing when Sundell turned and looked at Rosey. He looked harder at her because something caught his eye and didn't look quite right to him. He got up from the table and casually walked over to her and picked up her chin with his hand looking at the black eye. His face turned red as his blood pressure rose high and his temper got out of control.

"Who did that to you," he hollered in anger.

"It's nothing," said Rosey. "It's okay. I just fell and hit the corner of the table."

"I'm asking you who caused it to happen. I want to know now! Answer me!"

"I did it you ornery polecat! You want to make something of it?" said Payson.

Sundell turned fast and unhooked the thong on his gun, just as Dash jumped up from the table and yelled "You draw that gun on him and I'll kill you myself Sundell." He was already holding his 45 on the kid. Sundell hesitated looking at Dash's gun and took his hand off his gun, holding his palms up in the air.

"You know the rules. Leave your guns in here and settle it outside like men," said Dash. "You know the rules, Sundell. I'm not going to tell you again."

Sundell just looked at Dash with a mean scowl on his face. He wanted to take out Payson and end it the easy way with gunplay. But Dash was not having any of it.

Sundell unbuckled his gun belt and threw it hard onto the table. It made a loud crash and he was lucky the hair trigger on his gun didn't accidently make it go off. "Let's go outside", he said to Payson.

This time no line was drawn in the sand and there was no hesitation. Sundell jumped on Payson the minute he was in the clearing. They both went down in the dirt, clawing and grabbing at each other. They rolled over and over trying to get the better of each other. Payson grabbed Sundell by the hair and then grabbed his throat in an effort to choke him. However, Sundell broke free punching Payson in the gut knocking the wind out of him. Payson caught his breath and was up again. He picked up the horse shoeing hammer and threw it at Sundell. Sundell ducked and it missed him. They grabbed each other and rolled on the ground this time going under the horses that were tethered at the hitch rail. The horses bolted and moved around almost stepping on them. This fight went on for a long time before Sundell gave Payson his one, two punch knocking him down for the count. Sundell fell on the ground exhausted, trying to catch his breath. Dash called it a tie and Sundell got up to go after Payson again when Terry grabbed him, holding him back. "He had enough Sundell. It's over, go wash up and calm down," said Terry.

"Yeah, Sundell. Cool off and control that temper of yours. He had enough. It's all over," said Dash.

Sundell was very quiet that evening and said nothing to no one, including the girl. *This was her fault,* he thought. *I was fighting in defense of her honor. This girl is nothing but trouble for me. She better appreciate my efforts.*

He was still madder than a hornet when he grabbed his bedroll and went outside. Saddled the mare Stardust and left for the canyon. Sundell decided to sleep in the canyon tonight and cool off. Maybe he would be one step ahead of that stallion when he woke up early in the morning.

~~~ T2 Brand ~~~

As a favor to Sundell, JW decided to keep watch over the girl. He threw his bedroll down between her and the rest of the boys just as Sundell had done. Rosey noticed this precaution and was thankful for it. However, she was scared with Sundell so far away. JW noticed the girl was crying during the night and he felt bad for her. *Darn that Sundell,* he thought. *He should never have taken off and left the girl alone like this after all that has happened. I know he went after that black again. That cowboy is horse crazy! He'll never catch that black no matter what. Now I gotta watch the girl for him when she is his responsibility.*

~~~ T2 Brand ~~~

Sundell bedded down in the canyon and kept Stardust close by him in the temporary corral he made. He made sure she was tied down good so she wouldn't bolt or get away from him should the black stallion he called Shadow come around to try and free her again. This time he was using her as bait to lure Shadow in for the capture. Sundell knew this was the only way he would be able to capture Shadow. The mare was like sugar to that horse.

Sundell's thoughts turned to Rosey. He couldn't get her out of his head. No doubt about it, he was falling in love with her. *I'm only about eighteen going on nineteen,* he thought. *She can't be more than fifteen, a minor. I'm too young to get tied down with a girl and she is too young to get stuck with a drifter like me that will amount to nothing. I know what relationships are all about. I been around plenty of barmaids in the saloons after cattle drives. I know what men and women do together. At least I can remember that part of my life. I'm a cowboy and I know a lot about horses and livestock and breeding charts. Getting involved with this gang of outlaws was the only way I could save my life and survive. How would I know a girl got all mixed up in it along with a bank robbery? I'm really enjoying the charade pretending I have something physical going on with her. This gang of outlaws is so dumb it's not hard to put anything over on them. They all think I'm poking her when all the time I been protecting this girl for over a week now. I'm pretending I have a relationship going on with her, and now I'm finding out that I'm in real big trouble. I actually want to get physical with her. Damn my bad luck. I'm falling in love with Rosey but I won't dare violate a minor.*

Sundell's thoughts were suddenly interrupted when Stardust let out a whinny breaking the silence. *It's the black! He's near!* Thought Sundell.

He quickly got up and grabbed his rope. He loosened the thong from his gun just in case he needed it to shoot in the air. Opening the corral gate he checked that Stardust was tied tight. He was glad he thought to increase the height of the gate in case Shadow decided to jump it again. He hid in the bushes as the black approached. The horse could pick up Sundell's scent but thought what he was detecting was the cowboy's empty camp so he continued to approach the corral and his mare. He walked right into the corral and up to the mare when Sundell shut the gate.

Shadow reared and tried to jump the gate but found it too high to escape over it this time. Sundell had the black cornered. *Now what*, thought Sundell. *I've got to do everything I can not to get myself killed.*

From outside the corral, Sundell threw his rope over Shadow's head and secured the rope to a strong boulder. Then he started gently talking to the horse to gain his confidence. "Easy Shadow, boy. I won't hurt you, boy." The black reared up but the rope held him. "Easy boy. Easy Shadow boy." Sundell gently patted and touched the horse. The horse did not move in fear. So Sundell petted him some more letting the black get used to his touch. He did this for a long time staying very gentle with his hands as he petted and touched the horse. Sundell reached into his pocket and pulled out treats to offer and Shadow took them reluctantly. Shadow was beginning to respond to his voice and his touch. Sundell climbed out of the corral and went to his saddle bags to get some more treats for both horses. When he came back he treated Stardust first to let Shadow watch how it's done, then gave a treat to Shadow. He saw how Shadow liked the treat so he gave Shadow another treat. This seemed to be working well. He worked all morning on the horse, training Shadow not to be afraid of him and gaining his trust. Sundell's voice was gentle and kind.

He let Shadow rest for about an hour before starting on him again. Shadow nuzzled his mare and seemed to be affectionate towards her. They were getting reacquainted again after being separated for a week. Sundell gave Shadow as much time as he thought he needed with his mare. This seemed to be paying off.

However, as he watched the two horses caressing, his thoughts turned back to Rosey again. Sundell wanted to have that girl and he could feel the ache in his groin just thinking about her. When he grabbed Rosey and kissed her in front of the gang just for show, it also did something to him that he wasn't exactly expecting. He really wanted to have that girl. Virgin or not he wanted bad to test her waters. Sundell just shook his head at the thought of it. As bad as he wanted her, he just couldn't do it to her. After all she was a minor and in this territory, raping a minor could be a hanging offense depending on the judge and jury. Sundell knew for sure he had to keep his feelings in check when he was with Rosey. There was no reason to shame a decent really good girl. It wasn't going to be easy for him but he needed to behave when he was with her. It was times like these that he wished he really was an outlaw without a conscience to answer to. It wasn't like he could marry Rosey. She was much too young and innocent of the ways of men. In spite of what Dash thinks, I'll kill Payson if he touches her again.

Shadow had enough time with his mare. It was time for Sundell to start breaking the stallion's wild spirit through lessons of fear and respect. With a calm speaking voice he talked to Shadow then slipped the bridle on. Shadow was still full of spirit and fight. He gently slipped the saddle blanket on and Shadow reared throwing it off. Sundell did it again while talking gently to the horse. This time Shadow accepted the blanket. While continuing to talk to Shadow, Sundell slipped the saddle off the fence and onto the horse. Shadow was restless and scared. Sundell quickly set the cinch and secured the saddle. Shadow reared once but settled down to Sundell's touch and soft voice again. Sundell unlocked the gate pushing it open with his boot as he did a flying mount into the saddle. Shadow reared and bucked out of the corral screaming and kicking. Sundell had no idea where his bronc busting skills came from but he seemed to know exactly what he had to do. He stayed on the black for as long as he could and what a ride it was for his aching back. The stallion must have bucked for a half hour before he finally gave up and started walking. What a relief that was for Sundell. Sundell's tail bone felt like it was in his throat. It was going to take a lot more training to get Shadow to where Sundell wanted him, but if Sundell could get the black back to the cabin's corral he could continue to work with Shadow there.

Early that evening Sundell rode up to the cabin on Stardust leading Shadow on a rope.

"Hey, Dash," yelled JW. "Come out here you got to see this!"

Dash came out on the porch with all the others following behind him. He was in total shock.

"Get the hell out of here, this can't be!" he said.

"Hey, Dash," yelled Sundell. "I'm putting him in the corral. I don't want anybody touching him because I got to train him yet," said Sundell.

Dash was seeing it and yet he still couldn't believe his eyes. He just kept shaking his head. *Sundell said he has to train him yet,* thought Dash. *He even knows how to train a wild horse. Where did he ever learn the skills for that? Where did this cowboy come from?*

"Okay, everybody. You all heard Sundell. Nobody goes near that horse. I don't want any trouble from him, you hear? I don't want any of you boys getting killed!" said Dash.

"We hear you, boss," said Payson. "I ain't lookin' to get my ass stomped on by that killer. I can think of a lot better ways of dying. I might get real lucky if he kills Sundell."

"Hey you guys. Are you forgetting; I won that bet!" hollered JW.

Sundell rode up to the gate, opened it and put Stardust and Shadow into the corral. He proceeded to take care of them with water and feed. He would come out and brush them down after supper. As he walked up to the porch, Rosey came out the door to announce that supper was ready. Sundell came up on the porch, slipped his arm around her waist and pulled her in against him. He proceeded to passionately kiss her on the lips. The rest of the men just turned and went into the cabin for dinner pretending to ignore the public display of affection.

"I missed you, tootsie. Are you still mad at me?"

"I'll think about it and let you know later," said Rosey.

"Everything go all right while I was gone? Nothing happened that shouldn't happen?"

"Everything is fine, Sundell. JW was watching out for me."

"JW, huh? He didn't get too close to my girl, did he? He better not."

"No, silly. He just kept everyone else away."

"Well, all right then. Let's go in and eat."

"You will have to go hunting again, I'm running low on venison," said Rosey as they entered the cabin.

"What is this? Am I the only one supplying the fresh game for this bunch?" Sundell answered loud so everyone could hear.

"Newest member of the gang does all the hunting," said Payson.

"You're all fucking eating ain't you," replied Sundell to Payson. It seemed he just couldn't talk to Payson without getting pissed off.

"You got a big mouth, Sundell!" said Payson.

"Oh yeah? You want to try and shut it for me?"

"All right, you two. Don't start it up again Sundell, you just got back," shouted Dash. "Tomorrow we will *all* go hunting for game because the next day we got a big job to do. I'll tell you all about it after supper."

Chapter IV

THE NEXT BIG JOB

After the supper table was cleared, Dash gathered the men around to explain the next big job he had planned for them. They were going to the settlement of Canyon Diablo to rob the railroad payroll that was coming in on Friday of next week. The railroad was building a bridge across the canyon and it was taking them about ten years to build. They were getting pretty close to the end and they hired on several more workers to hurry the job along so they could meet the deadline to get it done. These new hires made the payroll job an even bigger haul than their previous jobs. Since it was known that the closest U.S. Marshall was one-hundred miles away this kind of job seemed really attractive to Dash. He aimed to get that fifty-thousand dollar payroll.

The Canyon Diablo settlement was built up as a railroad town for the men who were laying the tracks for the railroad. It was a rough town because it attracted outlaws, gamblers, and the worst kind of drifters. The town actually boasted about its five saloons, three brothels, several gambling parlors, two dance halls, and a couple of eating places, a dry goods store and Valin's Trading Post. All the buildings faced each other on the town's single rocky dirt road which was just off the railroad's right-of-way. That one main street was appropriately named Hell Street. Outlaws held up the stage line on a regular basis. The Gate of Heaven cemetery on top of the hill leading out of town was filling up with graves from fights and gun battles that happened every day in the town.

Canyon Diablo was two-hundred fifty-five feet deep. The railroad was pre-assembling the timber parts elsewhere and transporting them in by ox-team across the Little Colorado to Flagstaff and on to the Atlantic and Pacific Railroad Depot at Canyon Diablo as the railroad proceeded west.

"It will be a piece of cake robbing that stage," said Dash.

It was Dash's plan to rob the stage and get the payroll on the flats before the stage enters into the canyon. Sundell and Rosey were to hold the horses and keep them quiet while the rest of the gang flagged down the coach and robbed it. Dash decided since Sundell was the newest and youngest member of the gang, Dash needed to break him in gradually. Besides, it was the kid's job to keep watch over the girl, Rosey.

~~~ T2 Brand ~~~

Early the next morning they headed out for Canyon Diablo carrying enough supplies to sustain them for the trip out and back. Sundell was worried. Robbery was not his line of work and taking Rosey with them as a witness to the robbery was a big mistake. He knew it but had no say in the matter. At least their part of the job was to hold the horses. If they got caught, the charge against them would be no more than accessory to robbery. That thought alone pushed Sundell forward in pursuance of the plan. He prayed Rosey wouldn't take a stray bullet and get hurt. It was his job to see that she didn't get in the way, and he aimed to take good care of her. If it was up to him, he would have returned her to her home by now and taken his chances with the law. But it wasn't up to him. He was stuck in a bad situation for the time being.

When they stopped to make camp, Sundell noticed how tired Rosey looked. It was a long ride for a girl to do in one day. There was no doubt in his mind she was saddle sore. She was used to driving a freight wagon, not sitting a saddle all day long like a drover. He helped her down off Stardust as her exhausted body fell into his arms. He caught her and picked her up carrying her over to where the campfire was being set up. Sundell went back to Stardust and Shadow and unpacked the bedrolls. He came back and set them up for Rosey to lay down on.

"What's the matter with the freight wagon bitch? She can't take to travelling by horseback?"

"I told you before, Dash, she's a girl. This kind of travelling is hard work for her. She ain't used to it, so don't get on her case. I'll take care of her."

"You see to it that you do, Sundell. I don't want her holding us up." Sundell didn't answer, however, there was a scornful look on Sundell's face. He was tired too. It wasn't easy trying to take care of Rosey and keep up with this sadistic gang.

JW cooked up a quick meal when he noticed how tired Rosey was and how Sundell was holding her in his arms trying to relax her. Sundell felt relieved when he saw how fast JW took over the cooking. He shook his head at JW in a gesture of thanks. JW got the message. JW dished out the food and handed the first plate to Sundell who gave it to Rosey. She refused to eat it, so Sundell started feeding it to her.

"Come on. Eat or you will get weak." She started eating as he fed it to her.

"Here, Sundell. You better eat too," said JW as he passed a plate to Sundell. Sundell took it and set it down beside him. When Rosey finished he took his plate and wolfed it down.

"Is she okay?" inquired JW.

"Yeah. Just tired. She'll sleep well tonight."

"So long as you don't wake her, Sundell, ha, ha, ha."

"I won't wake her, JW. Not tonight, anyway. I'll need the rest myself."

~~~ T2 Brand ~~~

Morning came on fast. They ate a quick breakfast and hit the trail early. By the time noontime came they were already on the stagecoach road to Canyon Diablo. They found shelter behind some rocks off the shoulder of the road.

"This is a good place to keep the horses," said Dash. "Sundell you and Rosey keep the horses quiet and out of sight. The rest of us are going to block the road so the stage will have to stop. When it stops, we run out and take it over. I want that fifty thousand payroll and anything else you can get from the passengers if there is anybody on that stage."

They dismounted quickly throwing their horse reins at Sundell and Rosey to catch. They found a large log and a discarded railroad tie and dragged them across the road blocking it.

JW mounted his horse and back tracked along the stage road to watch for the stage and warn them of its coming. It was ten minutes later when he returned to warn them to get ready. The stage stopped when it approached the blockade. The Cogburn gang covered their faces with bandanas and ran out to meet the stage. From behind the rocks, Sundell shot the rifle out of the guard's hands and the guard put his hands up in the air. Dash looked back in surprise at the rocks not expecting Sundell to do that because Dash would have shot the guard dead on site if he saw the guard aim the gun at him. The driver and guard climbed down from the boot with their hands up. One male passenger exited from inside the stage. He was dressed like a gambler and the gang pulled a money belt off his waist. Dash climbed up on the driver's seat and threw down a strong box with the money in it. Payson shot the hasp off and the outlaws began filling saddle bags with the fifty thousand dollars. The outlaws ran back behind the rocks, grabbed their horses' reins from Sundell and Rosey then mounted and took off. As JW mounted, his horse reared knocking him down and it took off running away without him. Sundell saw it and went back to pick JW up on the back of Shadow when a rifle wined and a bullet caught Sundell in the left shoulder.

"I got one," screamed the guard.

JW mounted behind Sundell and they both took off following behind the rest of the outlaw gang. Blood oozed out of Sundell's shoulder and ran down over JW's hand as he held onto Sundell.

"Sundell! You're hit!" JW exclaimed.

"I know, but we can't stop now. We need to catch up with the gang."

They rode on for almost two hours catching up to the gang when the outlaws stopped to rest the horses. Sundell never realized his bleeding shoulder was leaving a bloody trail.

"Hey, Dash. Sundell caught some lead when he came back to save me from getting caught," cried JW.

Dash ran up to Shadow and caught Sundell as he fell off his horse to the ground. Rosey screamed when she realized Sundell was hurt.

"Shut up, Rosey. Stay quiet and get some rags over here fast. We got to stop the bleeding," said Dash. Rosey rushed and did as Dash ordered.

"Shit! Did you see that shot Sundell made from behind those rocks?" said Terry Jonas. "He took the rifle right out of the guard's hands. Point blank! Perfect shot! Wow! Never saw nothing like it! Expert shooting."

"We all saw it," remarked Dash. "It was good all right. Nice shot, kid. If it were me, I would have killed that guard's ass and fed it to the buzzards. Never leave a witness behind."

"Sundell. You saved my butt, kid. I would have been a goner if you didn't see me fall and come back for me. I owe you a debt of gratitude, cowboy."

"I couldn't see leaving you behind, JW," Sundell let out a moan from pain.

"Hey, Rosey. Get a canteen. Sundell needs a drink," replied Dash.

"I can try to stop the bleeding for now, Sundell. But I can't take the time to remove the slug. You'll have to wait till we get back to the cabin. Here take a sip of water," said JW taking the canteen from Rosey.

"I'll be okay. Let's get out of here before they catch up with us."

"All right boys. Mount up, we're heading out," said Dash.

~~~ T2 Brand ~~~

Sundell was hurting bad when they arrived at the hideout. Greg Wills dismounted and took Shadow and Stardust to the corral to take care of them and put them up. A couple of the gang members assisted Sundell into the cabin.

"Put him in my bunk," said JW. "Get some hot water and clean rags. Hurry!"

"Oh, God, this slug hurts. Get this lead out of me," moaned Sundell.

"Anybody know how to take a slug out?" questioned Dash.

"No," came back the answers from the gang.

"Leave it in him," replied Payson. "Maybe lead poison will finally kill him!"

"Shut up, Payson. Rosey! Can you do it?" asked Dash.

"I can't. It will make me sick and I don't want to hurt him. I'll try and find a knife though."

"Rosey," moaned Sundell. "There's a knife inside my right boot; use that."

JW ripped away the sleeve to Sundell's shirt as Rosey pulled the knife from Sundell's boot. She began washing away the blood as she and JW looked over the bullet hole. Rosey looked away feeling sick.

"I can't do this to him," she said.

"Get out of my way," said JW "and give me that knife. This is gonna hurt bad buddy. I'm no doctor. I owe you this much though."

"Just get the fucking lead out," moaned Sundell.

Rosey moved aside as JW took the knife from her and heated the knife blade in the lantern's flame. A chill ran up Rosey's spine when the blade glowed red hot. The rest of the gang gathered around to watch the procedure.

"Hand Sundell that bottle of whiskey," said JW. "He sure as hell will need it."

The whiskey bottle was handed to him. "Go ahead and drink it down before I dig in there, Sundell," said JW. "Go on drink some more."

"I don't want any more. Go ahead and dig," replied Sundell.

"Dammit! Drink some more of it kid," repeated JW. Sundell lifted the bottle and took a long drink. JW went into the wound with the knife and Sundell let out a loud holler coughing and almost choking on the liquor.

"Hurt him good, JW," said Payson. "I want to see his ass hurt real good. Ha, ha, ha."

"Shut up, Payson," said JW. "He's hurtin' badly all right and I'm not doing it on purpose."

"Oh my God! What happened? Is he dead, JW?" cried Rosey.

"Take it easy, Rosey. He just passed out. It's better that he did. I can get in there deep now and get that lead out. I can feel it now. No wonder it hurt so badly. It's resting up against a nerve. There it is! I got it!" JW dropped the lead into the wash pan of water. "Whew! He lost a lot of blood but the bleeding slowed and is stopping the minute I got the lead out. You got to help me get this wound packed. He is not out of danger yet. When the bleeding completely stops we got to hope to God it don't get infected. The knife is sterile. It shouldn't get infected but you never know about these things."

Rosey handed JW clean white rags. He packed the wound, wrapped and tied it tight. The wound stopped oozing and seemed to let up with the pressure on it.

"Somebody give me the canteen of water. Let's see if we can wake him up," said JW. Dash handed him a canteen of cool, fresh water. JW tipped it up to Sundell's lips and let it trickle. Sundell responded and woke up. "It's all over buddy. The lead's out. You need to sleep it off now. That slug was pressing on a nerve. No wonder it hurt so much." Sundell just smiled as he looked up at JW, let out a breath of air, and rolled over to go to sleep. Rosey seemed relieved shaking her head. *I'll check him through the night,* she thought.

Next morning Sundell was up early and walking around the cabin. Rosey made him sit down at the table while she fashioned his arm into a sling. It did feel much better that way and Sundell didn't complain.

When JW got up he wanted answers from the gang. "Why is it only Sundell came back to pick me up?" he questioned. "Not one of you came back to help me except for Sundell when my horse spooked and threw me. Were you all just going to leave me there to get caught?" JW was madder than a hornet.

"No sense in all of us getting caught," said Payson.

"None of us saw you fall," replied Greg.

"I heard the horse scream and rear but I didn't look back," said Terry.

"Lucky for you JW, that Sundell saw it all and went back to pick you up. Too bad he took a bullet for you," replied Dash.

"I'd of done it for anybody," replied Sundell. "If the law got hold of one of us we are all finished."

"Smart thinking, Sundell," said Dash. "I like a man with some brains in his head." Dash had a shit-eating grin on his face. He was ready to sit down and divide up some of the payroll. The rest they would bury for future use. This time he gave Sundell a cut of the loot intentionally leaving Rosey out on a share.

CHAPTER V

CHLORIDE GENERAL STORE

A couple days later—Sundell was feeling much better even though the bullet wound was tender and sore. He worked with Shadow and Stardust most of the day training them to come to him in answer to his whistle. He was an expert with horses as the gang witnessed time and again. After supper he worked again with the two horses late into the night and when he finally crashed into his bedroll everyone in the cabin was already asleep. It was an hour or so after midnight when he heard Shadow causing a disturbance out in the corral. It woke up Sundell and he noticed Rosey was missing so he went out to the corral to see what the matter was.

That is when he noticed Stardust was missing from the corral. No wonder Shadow was so upset. Both Rosey and Stardust were missing. It was his worst fears. He knew without a doubt, Shadow would follow the scent of Stardust. Sundell saddled up and mounted giving Shadow the lead to follow the mare's scent. They caught up with Stardust just outside the dangerous town of Chloride and who was riding her but Rosey just as he figured. Sundell whistled and Stardust stopped short as she was trained to do waiting for Sundell to catch up to her.

"Rosey! Just what do you think you are doing? You can't run away. Dash will kill me! Especially to Chloride, it's dangerous! It's a mining town. If they catch a girl out this late alone they'll rape you or worse!"

"Sorry Sundell but I'm not running away. I need some things at the general store."

"Are you crazy? Why didn't you just tell me what you needed? I'll get the stuff for you. What you are doing here tonight is insane! It could cause you your life! What is it you needed anyway that it couldn't wait until morning?"

"I can't tell you what I need, Sundell. I have to do this myself."

"What's so important that it can't wait till the store opens?"

"I can't tell you."

"I reckon you better tell me because I'm taking you back to the cabin right now."

"No. Please. You can't do that. I need to get some stuff."

"What stuff? Tell me dammit!"

"Female stuff; if you must know. My monthly has come."

"Your what? Oh no! No! Don't tell me it's what I'm thinking. I'm responsible for this too? Oh God!"

"Yes. My monthly is here. I'll need rags to take care of myself. I couldn't tell the gang that. I planned to slip away to the general store and break in and get what I needed to take care of myself."

"Suppose you get caught breaking in there? We will all be in big trouble. They'll find us all out! They'll find the hideout!"

"Then maybe you better help me get what I need so I don't get caught, cowboy."

"Oh good Lord. Help me." *This girl is more trouble then I need now.* He removed his hat and ran his fingers through his hair replacing his hat back on his head. "Okay, okay. We will ride up to the rear of the store. I'll break in through the back window and get you into the store. You gather what you need and get out fast. Don't waste any time."

"Okay," agreed Rosey.

The store window was a little higher up than Sundell first thought, however, he was able to break in by standing up on Shadow and climb in himself. He leaned out the window and pulled Rosey up and in through the window. The shades on the store front windows were already drawn down so Sundell lit a lantern and looked around the store. He picked up a box of shells to fit his gun and a bag of horse treats. Then he spotted some bolts of cloth.

"Hey, Rosey. There's cloth over here under the counter." Rosey came over immediately to look.

"I'll need something to cut it with," she said as she looked around. Sundell just gave her a hard look and pulled a bolt of white muslin out of the pile of bolts causing some bolts to fall to the floor.

"Come on, we're leaving, now." He handed the bolt to her and headed for the back window the way they came in.

"But Sundell. I don't need a whole bolt of muslin."

"Forget it. Let's just get the hell out of here," he answered.

If anyone caught them he didn't know what to say to them. They mounted their horses and silently walked them away from the store then picked up speed as they got farther away from the town. Sundell was sweating. That was harder and scarier to do this deed than running with the outlaw gang robbing stagecoaches. *The responsibility of taking care of this girl is becoming harder every day. This girl is nothing but trouble for me. I need to get her back home as soon as possible. I have enough trouble trying to take care of me,* he thought.

When they arrived back at the hideout, Sundell went right to bed after taking care of the horses. Rosey slipped behind the cabin to take care of her female needs and when she slipped back into her bed roll she noticed Sundell was already fast asleep. She couldn't help but laugh at how perplexed this cowboy was when she told him what she was up to. He was more scared and embarrassed then she was. She thought that was the funniest thing. He was right though. If she stopped to cut or rip that bolt into rags they may have gotten caught. She felt lucky that he was there to help her get away with her plan. She could always use the extra muslin for clean bandages on Sundell. Rosey found herself laughing every time she pictured the shocked look on Sundell's face when he realized what it was she was saying to him. He almost went into shock.

The next day Sundell was cleaning out the corral when Rosey walked up to the rail to watch him. When he saw the movement, he turned and looked at her with a totally straight face, then took a deep breath and let it out slowly. Rosey started to laugh.

"So tell me something, Sundell. How did you know where I went when you first found me gone? And how did you know I was gone?"

"Shadow told me you left. Then he followed the mare's scent. That mare ain't goin' nowhere without Shadow knowing about it."

"Does that mean I can't go anywhere on Stardust without you knowing about it?"

"Yes, ma'am. I reckon that's right."

"Darn," she said. "I can't even sneak away." Rosey walked back to the cabin.

Sundell watched Rosey walk back to the cabin and go inside. He couldn't help but laugh at her last comment. He had no intention of letting her out of his sight. If he lost her for any reason, Dash would kill him. She was a witness to the Brotherhood bank robbery even though he had no part in the robbery or the kidnapping.

Chapter VI

POSSE ON THE TRAIL

A posse was trying to follow a blood trail and horse tracks left by the outlaw gang that robbed the Overland Stage line of its railroad payroll. They were on the trail for a couple of days now when they were joined by the sheriff of Brotherhood and his deputy.

"Howdy. I'm Sheriff John Bridges and this is my Deputy Jim Cole. Your report on this robbery came in by wire and it said a young girl was seen with this band of outlaws you're chasing. It so happens I'm looking for the Dash Cogburn gang which kidnapped a young fifteen year old girl from my town. Did any of your men get a good look at the girl?"

"No, not that good. She was hiding behind some rocks with another gang member holding all their horses. We suspected she was pretty young, maybe about fifteen."

"Do you mind if we join you in the hunt for these outlaws? We have a big interest in these boys."

"Actually, Sheriff Bridges. We were just about to quit. I need to get back to my own office which is one hundred miles away from this settlement. However, if you want to continue the search from here, you're welcome to do so. We been following this trail of blood spots. One of the outlaws was hit and we thought maybe we would run across the body on the trail. But nothing yet. Looks to me like they are heading northeast towards the town of Chloride. Not sure though. You sure are welcome to take over where we are leaving off. If you should find them, wire us and we will be glad to help you bring them in."

Sheriff Bridges dismounted and looked at the blood spots on the trail.

"This is a pretty clear trail, providing it doesn't rain and wash away the evidence. I'd like to follow this trail even farther, providing I'm not stepping over the line into your jurisdiction. If they are the Cogburn Gang I'd like to arrest them with your approval."

"You got my permission to arrest them if it's the Cogburn Gang. But after you try them I want them next for the payroll job on the stage line."

"I totally agree to that sheriff. Thank you for giving me first dibs on this gang. I want to get the girl back. If they did any harm to her, you can have the ones I don't hang. Rape of a minor is a hanging offense in this here territory."

"I'm in total agreement with that. Any of you boys want to ride with Sheriff Bridges and help him get this gang?"

A few of the posse members agreed to stay on with Sheriff Bridges of Brotherhood and help him catch the gang. Sheriff Bridges moved on up the trail following the blood spots and horse tracks. He followed the tracks across the plains and up to another mountain range. They were headed towards Chloride all right. Sheriff Bridges decided to head on into town and see what he could find out in Chloride since it was getting harder to follow the trail of blood.

When he arrived in town there was a commotion going on in front of the general store. He decided to ride over there and listen in on what was going on. Apparently, someone broke into the store during the night through a back window. The only thing missing was maybe a bolt of white muslin fabric. The store owner knew this because when he opened up the store in the morning some bolts of fabric were laying on the floor in disarray and upon inspection he found one was missing. Now why would anyone want to steal just a bolt of white muslin fabric? That indeed was a very strange theft. There was only one bolt of white muslin in the store and now it was gone. The store owner did not notice that a box of gun shells and horse treats were also missing.

"That is a strange theft," said Deputy Jim Cole to Sheriff Bridges. "What would anyone want with a bolt of muslin except to make curtains for a window or white shirts?"

"I agree with you," replied Sheriff Bridges. "How about maybe using strips of muslin fabric to patch up a bullet wound after robbing the Overland stage?"

Deputy Cole turned suddenly and looked hard at the sheriff. "You don't think that's why they took it, do you? It sure makes a lot of sense to me now. You are really smart John."

"That's why I'm the sheriff and you are the deputy. I noticed that trail we were following leads all the way up that mountain over-looking this town. Why don't we all rest the horses, get something to eat and a room for the night. We can follow that trail up the mountain tomorrow morning. I've got a gut feeling about what's on top of that mountain at the end of that trail. If it's what I'm thinking, they will still be there tomorrow morning."

"Good idea, sheriff. I think we all need a good rest before any confrontations."

"Okay, boys. Put up your mounts and get some supper. We are leaving early in the morning on that trail again," said Sheriff Bridges. "Meet me right here at sunup."

~~~ *T2 Brand* ~~~

The next morning after breakfast the sheriff and his posse headed out of Chloride to scout that mountain trail they left the day before. It had rained during the night and the rain had washed away any of the blood that was remaining on that trail. It really didn't matter to the sheriff because he knew in his heart the Cogburn Gang was at the end of that mountain trail. He planned to arrest them all, try and hang any one of them that may have raped or violated the girl and any or all of them that killed the three bank clerks in the Brotherhood National Bank. This gang was in for some big trouble. Sheriff Bridges had a big enough posse to subdue the whole gang.

The mountain air seemed to be a might chilly compared to the temperature in the town of Chloride. However, about two thirds of the way up the mountain the posse came to what was a very clever setup. A cabin and a large corral with several horses. Smoke was rising up from the chimney of the cabin. It was still early morning and some of the cabin's inhabitants were not up and awake as yet.

The posse surrounded the cabin and hid out of sight in the vegetation. It's a good thing they did because someone came out of the cabin and walked over to the corral. The cowboy's arm was bandaged in white muslin over the top of his torn shirt sleeve. *That is my proof of the bloody trail I was following and the missing bolt of muslin,* thought the sheriff. When the cowboy approached the corral a beautiful shiny black stallion came running up to the fence and nuzzled the cowboy. Sheriff Bridges was taken aback at the beauty of that horse as the cowboy fed the horse some treats. The young man climbed through the fence and proceeded to take care of all the horses, filling the feed trough and checking their water supply.

A girl came out on the porch and called to him that breakfast was ready. The cowboy gave the girl a wave of acknowledgement. He headed back to the cabin and went inside. *Why that was Rosey Denver,* thought Sheriff Bridges. *Well I found the Cogburn gang, all right. Now to arrest them and get them back to Brotherhood for trial. This ain't gonna be easy.*

"Okay, boys we will move in slowly and I'll call them out. No shooting unless they shoot first. We don't want to hit the girl. Hey, everybody in the cabin! Throw your guns out the door and come out with your hands held high. We got you surrounded so you might as well give up. This is Sheriff Bridges."

Everyone in the cabin froze. They all looked at Sundell. "Sundell! Who is out there? Did you see anybody while you were out at the corral?" questioned Dash.

"I didn't see anybody, Dash. Shadow was a little restless but I didn't think nothing of it, he's been that way before."

"Dash! There's a posse out there," exclaimed Payson who was now looking out the window.

"Where the hell did they come from?" questioned Dash.

"We going out there or are we fighting?" asked JW with a frightened look on his face.

"Anybody that wants to go out there, go! I'm fighting it out," replied Dash."

Before Rosey realized what was happening, Sundell pushed over the kitchen table, grabbed her arm and pulled her down on the floor behind the table. The rest of the gang ran over to cover all the windows.

"Stay flat on the floor, Rosey, and don't get up for anything until it is all over. Do you understand? Don't *move* from behind this table!"

"Yes," said Rosey. Her voice trembled; she was scared to death. *What was going to be the outcome of all this,* she thought as she watched Sundell loading rounds into his gun.

"This may be your chance to go home, tootsie," smiled Sundell and he winked at her, turned and left to cover a window. Rosey suddenly realized what Sundell meant. The whole gang could all die, including Sundell, and she will be free to go home with Sheriff Bridges. *Oh my God, no!* thought Rosey. *Not Sundell. Please don't let Sundell get killed.* Rosey started to cry. She was so scared for Sundell, she was trembling with fear, almost going into slight shock.

The gun fight went on for over an hour. The Cogburn gang was taking a beating. Their ears were ringing from all the noise. JW got a shoulder crease, Greg Wills took a bullet crease in the leg, and Terry Jonas was shot dead.

"All right," called Dash. "We are giving up boys, we're out numbered. Sheriff, we're coming out" he called. "Don't shoot."

"Throw your guns out first and come out with your hands up," said Sheriff Bridges. The outlaws did so as the posse came running up into the clearing. One deputy collected the guns, the sheriff started hand-cuffing all the outlaws. There's one dead in here called out a posse member. Another deputy was saddling their horses when Shadow bolted at him. Sundell ran over to the corral with his hands cuffed.

"I'll saddle Shadow. He don't take to strangers. That bay called Stardust is Rosey Denver's horse. She's gentle. Saddle her for Rosey."

"All right mister, but if you make one move to escape I'll put you to sleep permanently!"

"I get your drift, deputy. I won't run. Not now," replied Sundell.

Sheriff Bridges went into the cabin and picked Rosey up off the floor. She was trembling and all shook up. "Are you all right, young lady?"

"Yes. What about Sundell? Is he dead?"

"Which one is Sundell?" inquired the sheriff.

"The youngest one," said Rosey.

"The young fellow is okay as near as I can see. He is at the corral saddling the horses with my deputy. Let's go young lady, we are taking you home. You don't happen to know what they did with the bank money, do you?"

"Yes sheriff. What's left of it is in the wooden box by the fireplace. I think the stage payroll is in there also. They didn't divide that one up yet."

"Thanks, Rosey." The sheriff opened the box and took out all the money putting it into saddle bags. He took it outside with Rosey. Sundell was walking Shadow and Stardust up from the corral. Two deputies were leading the other horses.

"Okay. Everybody mount. We are heading back to Brotherhood."

Sundell walked up to Rosey to help her mount. Rosey didn't like the fact that he was wearing handcuffs. She attempted to hug him around the neck and he stepped back away from her shaking his head before she could do it. Sheriff Bridges noticed it. *Something going on here with these two*, he thought with an evil glint in his eye at Sundell. Rosey was noticeably upset that Sundell rejected her as she mounted Stardust. She guessed immediately that the charade was all over between them. Sundell mounted Shadow and didn't look at Rosey. Then he turned to her with no emotion on his face.

"Stardust is yours now Rosey. I'm giving her to you. Take good care of her." Rosey's stomach rolled. *It was over. Sundell knows he is finished*, she thought.

"I will Sundell." Rosey answered teary eyed. The sheriff noticed that, too. There was definitely something going on between these two young ones.

It was a long ride back to Brotherhood, but the defeated gang knew better than to try to escape. There were too many members in the posse covering their every move. They stopped and camped for the night. The outlaws were kept separate from the posse in camp and guards were posted all around them. One of the posse members took the payroll back to the railroad office at Canyon Diablo. Brotherhood gets to decide the fate of the outlaws first before Canyon Diablo. Those that don't get hanged will serve a lot of time in Yuma prison on hard labor when their trials get completed.

Late afternoon the next day they arrived in Brotherhood, California to the surprise of the town's folk who gathered around for the excitement.

Chapter VII

JUSTICE IS SERVED

"All right you boys. Get down off those horses and head right straight through that door in front of you there," said the sheriff. "Head straight back through the office to those jail cells. Go on, get in there!" They did as Sheriff Bridges said and started to enter the cells.

"No wait sheriff," said JW. "You can't put Payson in the same cell as Sundell. They don't get along. They'll fight. They hate each other. Put me in with Sundell, sheriff."

"I don't care who goes in with who. Two of you go into each cell, now get moving or I'll shove you in there." The sheriff was getting angry. He had enough back talk from these boys on the ride back to town.

JW pushed past Payson and entered the first cell with Sundell. Payson scowled at JW. The sheriff closed the door and locked it. Dash Cogburn and Westley Payson took the second cell, Greg Wills took the third cell.

"Put out your hands and I'll remove the cuffs." Each outlaw in turn put their hands out through the bars and Sheriff Bridges removed the handcuffs.

"Sheriff, you haven't told us what charges you have against us. You can't just stick us in here without telling us what the charges are," said Sundell.

"All right, boys. I'm charging you all with bank robbery, the murder of three bank employees, kidnapping a minor, and you Sundell with the extra charge of rape."

"What! But sheriff, those charges are all false on me. I never robbed the bank, killed or kidnapped anybody. I never raped anybody either," said Sundell in surprise.

"Now you gonna try and tell me the rape was consent?" replied the sheriff.

"No, sheriff. I didn't do anything but kiss the girl. That's not rape. Ask the girl!"

"Rosey ain't around right now. She needs some privacy and needs to be with her father. She has had quite a trying time. You bruised her up pretty good, cowboy!"

"I'm telling you, sheriff. All those charges against me are false. Especially the rape charge. I didn't violate Rosey and I didn't bruise her up!"

"You speak your mind sternly young man. You always tell it like you think it is?"

"Nothing wrong with it sheriff. It gets things said in a hurry especially when the charges are false."

"He's lying, sheriff," said Payson. "The kid had himself one hell of a good time with the girl. Kept her to himself. Wouldn't let any of the rest of us near her. He slept with her every night and even woke up all wrapped around her and the fly on his pants was unbuttoned in the morning with his big balls hanging out!"

"Shut up, Payson," yelled Dash. "Don't you go ratting out on any of the boys'. Keep your mouth shut. Don't go giving out any information on anything." Payson walked away from the bars and plopped down in a bunk on the side wall of his cell.

"Sheriff, it's not true. I didn't violate or hurt the girl in any way. Just ask her."

"You'll get your chance to tell it to the judge in court, Sundell. Now you see that bunk on the side wall over there. That's yours. So go over there and get in it now and stay there. I don't want to hear another word out of you. You understand?"

Sundell went over and laid down in the bunk. Murder was a hanging offense but so was raping a minor. If he can't prove the charges as false, he was going to hang for sure. He made a real bad decision joining up with these boys and he was in big trouble for it. How was he ever going to get out of this predicament? It would have been better if this gang left him for dead when they found him on the trail.

<center>~~~ T2 Brand ~~~</center>

Rancher Mike Hammer was coming out of the general store when he noticed the sheriff and his posse bringing in the outlaw gang that was said to have robbed the Brotherhood Bank. The town's folk were saying the gang was apprehended up near the town of Chloride where they had a hideout in the mountains. He stopped and watched as the outlaws dismounted with their hands cuffed, and were pushed in the direction of the sheriff's office. The sheriff and his deputies were not exactly being kind and gentle with the boys. One of them stumbled when he was pushed but did not fall on the boardwalk. For some reason Mike thought one of the outlaws had a familiar face and he wondered where he might have seen him before. One of the deputies walked away and headed up the boardwalk towards Mike.

"Hey mister. Is that the Dash Cogburn gang you just brought in?" Mike asked.

"Sure is. We tracked them for three days. Every one of those bastards deserve to hang. They're murderers," he answered.

"There was a real young one with them. Do you happen to know his name, he looked familiar to me for some reason."

"Yeah. The kid's name is Sundell. Don't know anything else about him. But he's a bad one all right. He raped the girl they kidnapped. I can't wait to see him hang and kick *his* feet. If you'll excuse me, I need a drink bad."

"Much obliged, mister," said Mike.

Mike was concerned about the kid Sundell. He looked very much like the Sundell that brought him the horses from Yuma. He gave the kid Sundell two thousand dollars to take back to Yuma for the Flying T2 Rough Stock and Cattle Co. Now he was wondering if his contract got fulfilled and the money got back to that ranch. He rushed over to the telegraph office and sent a wire to the stock contractor inquiring if the money arrived safely back to the ranch. A couple hours later a wire came back for him that the money never arrived and neither did Sundell Lacey, son of the ranch's owner. This troubled Mike Hammer very much.

Mike went back to the telegraph office and sent another wire. He told the rancher the Dash Cogburn gang was picked up by the Brotherhood posse and thrown in jail on hanging charges and a young man named Sundell was in jail with them. This Sundell looked like the same young cowboy he gave the money to for the Flying T2 ranch. Mike thought the ranch should check this kid out in case he was impersonating their cowboy and stole the ranch money from him. An answer to Mike's wire came back immediately and it said four Lacey brothers were on the way to check it all out. They expected to arrive in about a week and hoped they would make it before the circuit judge arrived there for the trial.

~~~ *T2 Brand* ~~~

In the meantime, the sheriff was writing up all the paperwork on the prisoners and preparing for the arrival of the circuit judge and the trials. Sheriff Bridges received a telegram from the circuit judge saying that he would be a week late since he was finishing up a trial in another territory. This annoyed Sheriff Bridges because now he would have to feed these prisoners for a week or more and the town only allotted him enough money to feed two prisoners at a time. A jury had to be selected and a prosecuting attorney. The gallows had to be erected for hanging two at a time or all five at once. It was taking the better part of the week to get all the planning and preparations done. The prisoners were being fed bread and water during the day and beans at night since the money was so short. They were very hungry and getting grouchy and ornery.

It was early Thursday evening when the sheriff's two deputies came in and unlocked the cell Sundell and JW were occupying.

"Okay, JW move back against that wall and stay there. Don't move. Sundell come here up to the gate." The two boys did as they were told. They tied Sundell's hands behind his back and escorted him out the back door into the alley behind the jail.

"Hey! Where are you taking him?" shouted JW.

"None of your business!" said one of the deputies. They closed the cell door behind them, locked it and pushed Sundell through the back door into the alley behind the jail.

"All right, Sundell. The sheriff has paperwork to fill out on you and you are the only one he has nothing on. What is your last name?"

"I told him I don't have any other name but Sundell."

"You give us the answers we want or we'll knock them out of you. Now where are you originally from?"

"I can't tell you. I don't know," replied Sundell.

The bigger deputy back-handed Sundell across the face. "How old are you, kid?"

"I told the sheriff I really don't know. Maybe eighteen, I reckon."

The deputy punched Sundell in the stomach and he lost wind, coughing and gagging. He had a hard time catching his breath.

"Answer us! What town were you born in? Where you from?"

"I'm telling you the truth. I really don't know. I'd tell you if I knew."

The deputy punched Sundell in the face giving him a bad bruise, causing a black eye. Then he punched him again in the mouth cutting his lip. The ropes on Sundell's hands were burning his wrists as he struggled and ducked trying to defend himself from the punches. He felt dizzy and light headed then everything went black. Sundell passed out.

"Sundell better give us the answers we want," said Deputy Jake Horton, "or we are gonna end up being his worst nightmare. Let's put him back in the cell for now and we will try knocking some answers out of him again tomorrow."

The two deputies dragged his limp body back through the door and threw him on the floor of his cell to the shock of the on looking outlaw gang.

"What did you do to him?" yelled JW.

"Mind your own business you varmints, unless any of you know where he is from and can tell us what his last name is. We'll make him answer our questions sooner or later. The later we get the answers, the more unpleasant it will be for him."

"Wait a minute, you scum," yelled JW. He can't tell you anything because he has amnesia. He doesn't know anything about his past. Sundell can't even tell *us* where he is from."

"A likely story," said the taller deputy.

They locked the cell door and went into the office slamming the office door hard and not looking back.

JW ran up to Sundell and helped him struggle to get up onto his feet. Sundell was moaning and coughing. The bullet wound in his left arm had opened up during the confrontation and was bleeding. JW half dragged him over to the bunk where Sundell just collapsed into the bunk. He was breathing heavily and he was hurting badly.

Dash hung onto the bars looking into the cell. "How bad is he JW?" Dash asked.

"He ain't very good, Dash. They roughed him up real good. The kid's hurting."

"Those bastards. Nobody beats up on one of my boys and gets away with it. When I get out of here I'll kill both those bastard deputies."

"Maybe the kid deserved it, Dash," said Payson.

"None of my boys deserve to get beat up by the law, Payson. Not even you!"

"Just sayin', Dash."

"Don't say nothing, Payson. You said enough!"

"Sheriff. Sheriff," called out JW.

"What do you want, JW?"

"Give me a cup of water. I want a cup of water."

"You just had a cup of water half an hour ago."

"Come-on, sheriff. I want it for Sundell."

Sheriff Bridges walked over to the water barrel in the corner, took a cup off the hook and filled it with water.

"Okay, here. But you're only getting one. No more water until tomorrow morning."

"Thanks, Sheriff. You tell those deputies of yours to lay off of Sundell or there will be hell to pay."

"What did they do to him?"

"They roughed him up pretty bad, sheriff!"

"I told them to try and get answers out of him. I didn't tell them to beat him up."

"Maybe you should have put it in writing for them, sheriff. Can those goons of yours even read?" replied JW.

"That's enough, JW."

"Hey sheriff," hollered Dash. "What about some supper? We're all starving."

"I'll send out for some beans."

"Beans again! How about something solid? We're all getting the runs from too many beans."

"The town doesn't pay me enough to feed more'n two prisoners. You're lucky you are getting beans."

JW held up Sundell's head and gave him small sips of water. Then he took off Sundell's bandanna and wet it down washing the blood from his swollen face and lip with it.

"Just take it easy, kid. You'll get through this. You've gotten through being roughed up before." Sundell just moaned as he regained consciousness from the cold wet water. The night seemed very long as the shadows moved across the dark jail cell. Sundell had a very rough night tossing and turning as sleep would not come.

~~~ *T2 Brand* ~~~

It was noon on Friday when the Lacey brothers arrived in Brotherhood, California. They wasted no time getting there, riding almost all night, every night, with very little sleep. They had a brother that never showed up at the ranch and they needed to check out this Sundell who was in jail with the Cogburn gang in case he was their missing brother. TJ tethered his horse at the rail in front of the sheriff's office.

"You boys wait here while I go in to see the sheriff. I don't think he will let all of us in to see this Sundell," said TJ the oldest brother. The brothers dismounted. "Okay, TJ, we will wait right out here for you," replied Cimarron.

TJ walked into the sheriff's office and he could hear a fresh pot of coffee bubbling on the stove. The aroma smelled great. Sheriff Bridge's was doing paperwork and the deputies were out and about the town.

"Howdy, sheriff. My name's TJ Lacey from Yuma. I'm a rancher and I own a spread about ten miles outside of Yuma." TJ offered his hand to shake. Sheriff Bridges took his hand for the shake.

"I'm sheriff Bridges. What brings you to my town cowboy, business?"

"I guess you might call it ranch business, sheriff. I'm looking for a cowhand named Sundell and as I understand it, sheriff, you got one named Sundell locked up in your jail."

"What do you want with him, mister?" Sheriff Bridges eyed him suspiciously.

"Well for one thing the man had two thousand dollars of my ranch money on him which he was bringing back to me from a livestock sale. Only he never returned to the ranch with the money. I'm out looking for him."

"You think the Sundell in my jail may be the man you're looking for and you think he may have stolen your ranch money?"

"Don't know sheriff. I'd like to get a good look at him and see if I can identify him as the Sundell I'm looking for."

"All my prisoners have hanging offences against them and Sundell has more than one against him. No one is allowed in to see these prisoners."

"You got to let me in to get a look at him, sheriff. It's important to me."

"We're waiting on the circuit judge to get here, try them, and hang them. No one is allowed in there."

"The law says an attorney is allowed in there, sheriff, and I'm a legal attorney, here are my credentials." TJ threw his credentials on the desk in front of the sheriff. Sheriff Bridges looked them over.

"You are an attorney all right! But you are still not allowed in there unless you are representing Sundell in a court of law."

"Okay, I'll represent him. So let me in there to look at my potential client, sheriff. Sounds to me like you already got him tried and convicted. Remember, sheriff. These boys are innocent until proven guilty." Sheriff Bridges sighed.

"All right, but you get only five minutes in there with him. Let's go." The sheriff picked up the keys from a peg and unlocked the door to the room of cells.

Sundell was asleep on his bunk facing the back wall when they walked in. TJ looked at the sleeping figure. *That's the color of my brother's hair all right*, he thought.

"I need to see his face, sheriff," he said.

"Hey, JW. Is Sundell sleeping?"

"Yeah, sheriff."

"Wake him up. Give him a good shake."

"No sheriff, that ain't fair. He's only been sleeping two hours. He had a very rough night after your two baboon's got through with him."

"I said wake him up. You hear me! He has a visitor."

JW proceeded to wake up Sundell very gently. Sundell was very slow at stirring. He moaned, and stretched then looked up at JW with confusion on his face.

"You got a visitor, Sundell," said JW.

"Who would be visiting me? I don't know anybody," replied Sundell. Sheriff Bridges interrupted the statement.

"Sundell!" he shouted out. "Look over here at the cell door. Somebody wants to see your face. Don't argue with me just do as I say and look over here."

Sundell looked at the cell door with a blank expression on his face and when he did, TJ was startled.

"Let me in there, Sheriff. That man is my brother! I want to go in there and see him. I'm his attorney, remember!"

"All right. Take it easy mister. Since you are an attorney and representing him, I'll let you in there. Maybe now I'll get some answers on this kid. JW back up against the wall and stay there. Don't move while I let this man into the cell. If you move a muscle, I'll fill you with lead." JW did exactly as he was told. TJ quickly ran into the cell and up to the bunk kneeling down. Dash and the rest of the gang stood up and walked over to the bars looking on in curiosity.

"Sundell! What's going on here? Why are you in jail and what happened to you? Why are you all beat up?"

"Who are you mister? Do I know you?"

"Sundell! I'm your brother, TJ. How come you don't know who I am?"

"He's got amnesia, mister. He can't remember any of his past," offered JW. "As for the bruises and cuts, the sheriff's two gutless baboons roughed him up last evening trying to get him to answer their questions."

"I got a brother?" questioned Sundell.

"You got four brothers," answered TJ. "The other three are outside waiting for me to identify you and come out. Whatever his bail is sheriff I'll pay it."

"No bail," said Sheriff Bridges. "He will hang high with the rest of his gang members."

"Wait a minute, sheriff. Sundell is not a part of any gang! What are the charges against him?"

"Let's see. Bank robbery, murder of three bank employees, kidnapping, and rape of a minor. Sundell is the only one with rape charges against him."

"Something wrong here with these charges, sheriff. Sundell would never rape a woman, let alone a minor. He wasn't raised like that."

"He will hang high and kick his feet with the rest of them."

"I'm his attorney now, sheriff. You can't pass judgement on a man before he is tried. And another thing. It's against the law to beat up prisoners in custody. I'll get to the bottom of what's going on around here. I also want to know what happened to the two thousand in ranch money he had on him. Who took it? You?" Dead silence entered the room as everyone looked around at each other.

"There was nothing on him when we brought them all in. Whatever extra money they had must be buried somewhere or spent. All Sundell had on him was a pocket knife and his gun. The recovered payroll from the stage robbery went back to the railroad in Canyon Diablo where it belonged. What was left of the bank money they robbed from here went back to the Brotherhood Bank. There was no other money that I know about."

When Dash overheard that the missing money amounted to two thousand dollars in ranch money his ears picked up fast. The first thing he wanted to do was choke some answers out of Payson and find out if he took money from those saddle bags on the dead horse.

"Your five minutes is up, TJ. It's time to come out of there. Let's go."

"Sundell. I'll be back tomorrow. I'm your attorney now. You're not going to trial without me. Don't say or admit to anything without talking to me first. I'll get to the bottom of this whole thing. Just take it easy kid."

"Hey sheriff. When are we getting something solid to eat? We're all starving and getting weaker every day?" hollered Dash. With that, TJ turned suddenly and looked at Dash.

"When was the last time you boys were fed?" he asked.

"We been getting a piece of bread and a cup water for breakfast and lunch and beans for supper since we been in here. That's it! We're all getting the runs from the beans and getting weaker every day. We're starving to death!"

"Sheriff! It's against the law **not** to feed incarcerated prisoners. You feed these men solid food right now!"

"I don't have the money to buy dinners for them. The town only allots me enough money for two prisoners. I'm dividing up the money they give me five ways for rations."

"I'll pay for five dinners for tonight. I'm ordering five steak dinners and my brothers will pick them up for you and I'll pay for them. And another thing sheriff. I want a doctor in here, right away, to look at Sundell and patch him up."

"What! I don't have money to pay for a doctor either!"

"Then maybe you should keep your no-account, knuckle-busting deputies away from the prisoners. Get a doctor in here and I'll pay for him, too. Do it now! You hear? I can bring charges against you and your deputies and have your badges."

TJ went out onto the boardwalk and told his brothers Sundell was in big trouble. He sent them down to the café to get five steak dinners for the prisoners and gave them some money to pay for them. Sheriff Bridges sent one of his deputies to fetch the doctor for Sundell.

"TJ. While you're here come into my office and help me get the answers I need on Sundell's paperwork, since you claim he is your brother. I still have to fill out routine paperwork on him." TJ followed Sheriff Bridges back into the office.

"I'm assuming his last name is Lacey, same as your last name. Am I right?"

"That's right sheriff." The sheriff wrote it down on the form.

"Now I need his age, his weight, his height, place of birth and any other information you can give me on him."

"He's eighteen, sheriff, almost nineteen. Weight, one hundred seventy five, height five foot eight inches. He was born on our ranch, so I guess Yuma, Arizona would be where he is from."

"He looks too young to be eighteen. I would have thought he was closer to sixteen. Guess now I will have to try him as an adult. If he's proven guilty he will hang for raping a minor. This young man is in big trouble. Anything else you can tell me about him?"

"Sundell works for me as a cowboy, sheriff, on the Flying T2 Rough Stock and Cattle Ranch. That's where he was working up until a month ago, then he was assigned the job to deliver some horses to Mike Hammer, a rancher outside of Brotherhood. He is one darn good cowboy, sheriff, and an even better horse wrangler. When it comes to knowing and training horses, he's the best."

"I understand he is fast with a gun, TJ. A man like that can be pretty dangerous and considered a gunslinger."

"He is fast all right sheriff, but all of us brothers are fast. We learned from our father Tom Lacey aka the Nevada Kid. In fact we brothers have contests against each other back behind the barn and my brother Cimarron proved to be the fastest of us all."

Just then TJ's three brothers walked into the sheriff's office carrying dinner plates each filled with huge steaks and lots of vegetables. TJ, Sheriff Bridges and Deputy Horton took the plates back to the prisoners in the cells and handed out the dinners.

"It's about time we got a good meal in this dump," replied Dash. "Thanks a lot, mister."

Sundell struggled up into a sitting position as JW handed him a plate of food. "Eat it all Sundell, you need to get some strength back."

~~~ T2 Brand ~~~

Dr. Ingalls walked into the sheriff's office while the sheriff was in the back room collecting empty dinner plates from his prisoners. "Somebody in here need a doctor?" he questioned when he saw TJ.

"Yes, doctor. My brother Sundell in the first cell on the left. I'll pay you whatever the cost for your services."

"What seems to be the matter with him?"

"He has amnesia to begin with and then the two deputies here roughed him up pretty good trying to get answers out of him that he couldn't give. I'd appreciate anything you can do to help him out."

"Okay, I'll take a look at him."

TJ and Sheriff Bridges watched and waited as the doctor examined Sundell.

"What's the story doc?" asked TJ.

"Yeah he had amnesia all right. But by his eyes it looks like it's clearing up. Maybe the punch in the face brought back the memory. Can you remember anything young man?"

"TJ what's going on? Why is the doctor here?"

"I reckon his memory is coming back, doc. He didn't know who I was yesterday. Doc's checking you out Sundell. Can you remember anything about the past?"

"I remember my horse slipping on a soft shoulder and falling off a high mountain trail. It hit a ledge jutting out and threw me off on the mountain's ledge. I hit my head on a rock and I guess I passed out."

"Keep going. What else do you remember, kid?"

"I found a receipt in my pocket from Mike Hammer that said he paid me for the Flying T2 contract but I didn't have the money on me. I checked my saddle bags where I put the money and they were empty. I checked the ravine and under the horse but I couldn't find the money. It was nowhere around. I don't know what happened to the two thousand in ranch money, TJ. I felt very confused and dragged my saddle to a clearing and laid down to take a rest. I was real tired."

"He is getting his memory back, doc. He didn't know any of that yesterday. Can you remember anything after that, Sundell?" said TJ.

"Yeah, Dash Cogburn came by with his boys and a girl that told me she was their captive. He offered to feed me and take me with them or leave me to die on the trail. So I joined up with them to stay alive. I found myself being protective of the girl captive, also."

"Did you rob the Brotherhood Bank with them, kill three employees and kidnap the girl, Sundell?" asked Sheriff Bridges.

"Not that I know of, sheriff," replied Sundell.

"We picked him up on the trail after the Brotherhood bank robbery, sheriff," offered JW. He had nothing to do with the robbery or the kidnapping of the girl."

"Shut up, JW," yelled Dash. "He's a part of this gang and goes down with the rest of us. So keep your mouth shut."

"So sheriff. That clears him of the charges you are holding against him," injected TJ. "Your charges are all false."

"Not exactly, TJ. He is also charged with the rape of a minor. That is a hanging offense. There are witnesses on that charge and you said he's eighteen, so I have to try him as an adult. There's also the matter of accessory to the stage robbery."

TJ didn't know what to answer. This rape charge was serious. How was he ever going to clear the charge? Was this girl a creditable witness or would she only make matters worse for Sundell. He had no way of knowing. The girl was the key witness to it all.

"I'm going to give Sundell something to make him sleep tonight," said the doctor. You can question him more in the morning. I think he's had enough stress for now. I want you all to leave him alone for now. He does have a slight temperature. I'll stop by tomorrow morning and check him out again. Now everybody get out while I give him a sedative."

~~~ T2 Brand ~~~

Sundell's temperature increased during the night as the bullet wound on his shoulder began festering. The doctor never knew he had a bullet wound and never checked it. After the beating he took in the back ally of the jail the wound had opened up and got dirty. It was inflamed and getting infected.

Meanwhile, Dash was getting anxious about the two thousand dollars in ranch money. He was positive now that Payson stole it from Sundell's saddle bags before he met up with the gang in town. He decided to approach Payson during the night and force him to tell where he hid the money.

The quiet argument between Dash and Payson woke up JW. He tried hard to listen in on the argument and found out that Dash was accusing Payson of stealing the ranch money from Sundell's saddle bags. JW couldn't believe it when he heard Payson give in and admit to Dash that he stole the money and buried it. However, Payson never revealed where he buried the two thousand. Dash was furious with Payson because he wanted his share and a split.

When Sundell let out a moan in his sleep it brought the sheriff into the cell room to check out the noise. Dash backed off from Payson never getting an answer as to where he stashed the cash.

"What's going on in here?" exclaimed the sheriff. JW got up out of bed and walked over to Sundell.

"It's Sundell sheriff. Something is wrong. He is moaning in his sleep." JW touched Sundell's forehead and it was burning up. "He's burning up with fever, sheriff. I think he needs a doctor."

"Get back against the wall, JW. I'm coming in there to check it out." Sheriff Bridges came into the cell and sure enough, JW was right. "I'll get the doctor JW. He *is* burning up. Hope he doesn't have anything contagious to pass on to the rest of us." The sheriff locked the cell and left in a hurry.

"Is that all you're worried about, sheriff! You have no compassion at all!" hollered JW at the sheriff's retreating back. The sheriff closed the door hard.

"Hey, JW. Good job at distracting the sheriff," said Dash. "Maybe we can do a three way split."

"I didn't do it as a distraction, Dash. Sundell is really sick."

"Well, if he dies in his cell, it will save him a hanging. That's the easy way out."

"That's not funny, Dash."

"It wasn't meant to be funny, JW."

Sheriff Bridges came back with Dr. Ingalls and TJ following on his heels. He unlocked the cell and the doctor ran into the cage.

"Wow! He's burning up with fever all right. I wonder what happened. He was all right when I left him earlier. There's an infection somewhere."

"An infection?" replied JW. "Hey doc. Check the bullet wound on his left arm."

"This man has a bullet wound? Why wasn't I told that when I first examined him?" Dr. Ingalls cut away the shirt sleeve to check the arm. "There it is. The wound has been scraped open and has dirt in it. It's infected. Now why wasn't I told about this?"

"I guess everyone forgot it was there, doc. He never complained about it. It must have broken open when he was beat up in the back alley," said JW.

"The treatment of the prisoners in this jail is unacceptable," replied TJ.

"I knew he had a bullet wound but I thought it was fixed," said Sheriff Bridges. "That's the bloody trail I followed to the hideout."

"He caught lead at the stage robbery when he came back to pick me up," answered JW. "My horse bolted and threw me, then ran away. Sundell came back for me and picked me up. That's when he caught a bullet. We rode double back to the hideout and he bled most of the way back. I dug out the lead and Rosey patched it up afterwards. Last time the bandages were changed, it was doing fine."

"Well it's not doing fine right now. It's infected. I'll clean it out and medicate it. That's about all I can do. I'll give him something for the fever and check on him tomorrow. Hopefully, it will start mending again. It will leave a bad scar on him. By the way, sheriff. There will be no trial on this man until I say he is well enough to go through with it.

"It's okay, doc. I'm trying the others first. We'll try him last now that the only charge against him is rape and accessory to stage robbery."

"You're gonna find out, sheriff, that Sundell didn't rape that girl, because I aim to prove it. I told you he wasn't raised like that. None of us were."

"Right. Now you're gonna tell me the sons of that desert scorpion the Nevada Kid were raised with class? We will see what comes out in the trial," replied Sheriff Bridges.

"When this is done and over, sheriff, I'll make you apologize for slandering the Lacey name," said TJ. Sheriff Bridges ignored the threat.

"All right. Everybody out of the jail. You prisoners go back to sleep. I don't want to hear another sound out of you until morning."

~~~ *T2 Brand* ~~~

At breakfast the next morning TJ explained to his three brothers what happened during the night.

"The sheriff came and got me and the doctor during the night. Sundell's fever was very high. Evidently the bullet wound he had caught a few days before they were apprehended became infected. Doc had to clean it out and medicate it. I'm hoping today the fever will be down and he will be okay."

"Those deputies had no cause to beat him up in the back alley like that," said Tyler.

"They didn't know he had a bullet wound under his shirt sleeve. He had a different shirt on. No bullet hole was in the shirt sleeve to give it away."

"Still there was no call for their actions," said Gage.

"They don't know it yet, but I'm gonna use the deputy's' actions against them for leverage in the court trial. After breakfast Gage, you and Tyler take five good breakfasts up to the jail for the prisoners. Here's some money."

"What do you want *me* to do, TJ?" questioned Cimarron.

"I want you to go over to the stables and take care of Sundell's new horse Shadow. Sundell thinks the world of that horse. See to it all our horses are fed and well taken care of, also. I don't trust the people in this town. They are far too eager to hang the innocent."

"What are you gonna do, TJ?"

"Well Cimarron. I reckon I'll go over to that freight office and check on my only witness, this Rosey Denver. I want to get some straight answers out of her. I'll need her testimony to clear Sundell. One more thing boys. Stay out of trouble while we are in this town. The sheriff indicated to me that he wasn't exactly thrilled that we are the sons of the Nevada Kid." TJ grinned and winked at his brothers before he left the Hash House Cafe. He went straight up the boardwalk to the Denver Freighting Company.

~~~ T2 Brand ~~~

When the Lacey boys finished their errands they met back at the café and then headed into Dave's Barber Shop for haircuts and shaves. Cimarron came out of the barber shop first and sat on the bench out front. Tyler came out second and joined him on the bench. Then Gage came out last.

"What are you two looking at so hard?" replied Gage.

"You probably wouldn't understand little brother." remarked Cimarron.

"Try me," said Gage.

"Well, all right." replied Cimarron. "You see those two girls across the street looking into the millenary shop window?"

"Yeah, so what?"

"Well the one in the yellow dress bent over real far and we got to see a little more leg rather than just an ankle."

"Sundell is in jail and all you two can think about is girls! What's the matter with you?"

"He doesn't get it, Tyler."

"He's too young, Cimarron."

"Actually, Gage. We got to see a little bit more than just leg. You get it now?" asked Tyler.

"I got it the first time, you desert lizards," replied Gage.

"Hey, Ty. What do you say we go over there and introduce ourselves? Maybe they would like to join us for dinner tonight. This town is so boring. I want the one in the yellow dress."

"TJ said for us to stay out of trouble and girls are nothing but trouble," said Gage.

"Little brother. Why don't you go find something to keep you busy. Like go back down to the stables and brush down all our horses," giggled Cimarron.

"I know. You're just trying to get rid of me."

"You got the hint, little brother. So do us a favor and go get lost for a while," laughed Tyler.

"I'll get lost all right. I want nothing to do with you two when you get into trouble." Gage stood there and watched his two older brothers cross the street towards the girls. *Nothing but trouble coming. I can see it all now,* he thought.

"Good afternoon, ladies. It's a beautiful day today, is it not? Sun is shining and a slight cool breeze just strong enough to roll a tumble weed out on the desert." The sisters turned around and looked over the two cowboys tipping their hats to them.

"Is that supposed to be a fresh joke or something, cowboy?" inquired the girl in the yellow dress.

"No ma'am. Just makin' conversation. May I introduce myself? I'm Cimarron Lacey and this here fellow is my brother Tyler Lacey."

"Oh, brothers. What a co-incidence because we are sisters," said the girl in the yellow dress.

"May we ask what names you pretty girls are going by?" asked Cimarron.

"My name is Jeanne Compoli and my sister is Mary Lee."

"Two beautiful names for two beautiful girls. Are you girls from Brotherhood?"

"Actually, our father has a ranch about eight miles out of town so we are from Brotherhood but we live at the ranch," replied the girl in the blue dress. Where are you gentleman from? Why are you in town?"

"We are from Yuma, Arizona. We are in town on ranch business," replied Cimarron.

"We are working cowboys," said Tyler.

"By the way you wear your guns makes a girl wonder," replied Jeanne. "You look more like gun slingers to me. Cowboys don't wear their guns that low at least the cowboys on our ranch don't. Come on Mary Lee lets go into the store and look at more hats."

"Wait a minute girls. We would be happy to buy you each a new hat and take you to the café for coffee or tea and a desert. What do you say? How about it?"

"Sounds to me like a con-job," said Jeanne.

"Well maybe a little bit," replied Cimarron. "You see we don't know anybody in town, miss, and we have a couple hours to kill and we would love some company to talk to over coffee. What do you say?" Cimarron put his arm out for Jeanne in the yellow dress to take hold of and she did so. Tyler offered his arm to Mary Lee in the blue dress and the four walked down the boardwalk towards the Brotherhood Hash House.

The two couples spent an hour or more in the hash house, the girls drinking tea and the cowboys drinking coffee and eating scones. They were becoming very friendly and very cozy with each other, then decided to walk back down to the hat shop. The boys promised the girls new hats and followed through on their promise. Cimarron decided he liked the color yellow much more than he realized and bought Jeanne a yellow bonnet with red roses on it to match her dress. Tyler bought Mary Lee a blue bonnet with feathers and a blue bird on it.

"We want to thank you boys for the beautiful hats, but we really must be getting on back to the ranch now," said Jeanne.

"Oh no. You gotta go so soon?" replied Cimarron.

"I'm afraid we do," said Mary Lee. "Pa will be expecting us. If we don't show at a certain hour he sends the ranch foreman and a couple hands out to bring us back. He doesn't like us in town alone for too long."

"I can surly see why," replied Tyler.

"You can walk us to our buggy at the livery if you would like," said Jeanne.

"Okay. We'll do that. All right Ty?"

"Sure why not," said Tyler.

"How about the four of us go on a nice picnic tomorrow down by that lake we saw on the way in to town?" suggested Cimarron.

"I don't think so," said Jeanne. "We don't know you well enough to do something so private with you by the lake."

"Come on," said Cimarron. "We're not bad guys. We been with you for two hours. Can't you tell by now?

"Well, okay, I guess. We will meet you here in town at the hat shop around noon. We won't tell pa, because our pa won't like us doing a picnic with strangers so soon."

"Okay. At noon then." They reached the livery and their buggy was ready.

"Before we help you into that buggy may we have a little kiss?"

"No Cimarron. We don't know you boys that well. It's not proper."

"Sure it is, girls. You need to give us a thank you kiss for the hats. It's not right if you don't thank us."

"Since you put it that way, I guess it's okay. Right Mary Lee?"

"Okay, Jeanne."

The two girls offered their cheeks for a peck but the boys took the girls tightly in their arms and kissed them soundly on the lips. Both girls were in shock and refused to admit they liked it. These cowboys were over-stepping their bounds. If their pa found out about this, they were in for a lot of reprimand. As they talked on the way home in the buggy they decided not to tell anyone what happened. Perhaps they better cancel the picnic plans for tomorrow. As much as they liked these two boys, the cowboys were a bit too fast for them. Goodness knows what these boys will do to them on a private picnic by the lake. Could they trust them or not. These cowboys seemed to know exactly what they were doing and how far they wanted to go. The girls would decide tomorrow whether to stand them up or not.

Mary Lee did not want to stand up Tyler, but Jeanne being a little more cautious and level-headed wanted to stand up Cimarron. They would figure out what to do after a good night's sleep. Mary Lee slept sound that night, however, Jeanne could not stop thinking about Cimarron and the feel of that unbelievable passionate kiss.

He certainly was experienced at kissing. The best thing she could do was stand him up because if she didn't, she was in awful big trouble with her emotions. Cimarron's kiss turned her emotions on so fast she found herself unable to control her spinning head. This was one good looking, charming cowboy. He could turn her on in no time flat. None of the cowhands working for her pa's ranch could do this to her. They all tried and failed. Jeanne was afraid she met her match. What a soul mate Cimarron would make. She knew for sure she would have to stand him up because she didn't know exactly what this man's intentions were all about. She would have to know him a lot better before she could allow herself to give in to his charms or his kisses again. Jeanne fell asleep with a big smile on her face wondering what this pretentious cowboy would do if he was stood up on a date. It would be very interesting to find out.

CHAPTER VIII

JUDGMENT BY TRIAL

"Let's go boys, get up and get dressed." TJ was waking up his brothers early in the morning. "Come on we're going for breakfast early. The judge is in town. He arrived last night. The trial for Greg Wills is at ten o'clock this morning. I want to be there for the outcome of this trial. We need to see how this court operates."

Moans and groans were coming from the beds of Cimarron and Tyler. "Do we have to go, TJ? We got plans for lunch today."

"Yes you have to go. What are you two up to now?"

"Aw. We're going on a picnic with a couple girls from a ranch outside of town."

"If the trial is not over by noon, you can always leave early. Now get up and get dressed. Besides. I told you to stay out of trouble and girls are trouble."

The Lacey brothers washed up and dressed for the first trial. They headed down to the Hash House for breakfast. They finished breakfast with little time to spare and headed down to the court house for the trial of Greg Wills. The trial lasted all morning and ended just before noon time. The jury found Greg guilty of three counts of theft and convicted him to four years of hard labor in Yuma Prison. A wire would be sent to the Tumble Weed Wagon to pick up the prisoner and transport him to Yuma Prison.

TJ and Gage headed to Denver's Freighting Company to see if Rosey was back from a freight run. The clerk informed him that she was still not back. TJ was concerned if she would arrive back in Brotherhood before Sundell's trial came up. She was the only witness that could clear the rape charges against his brother. He needed to question the girl and get all the answers he needed to present his defense case. Was she deliberately being detained so as not to testify on the case? TJ was clearly concerned but didn't let his fears show to the other brothers.

Cimarron and Tyler rushed over to the hat shop to meet Jeanne and Mary Lee Compoli for their lunch date. They arrived just a few minutes before the buggy came into town. Something was wrong! Only one girl, Mary Lee, was in the buggy at the reins.

"Mary Lee where is Jeanne?" asked Cimarron.

"I'm sorry but she changed her mind about your lunch date, Cimarron," replied Mary Lee. Tyler climbed into the buggy and took the reins from Mary Lee. "We got fried chicken for our lunch Tyler. I make great fried chicken. Just wait until you taste it."

"That ain't fair! Blurted out Cimarron. "Why did she change her mind Mary Lee? What happened? Did I say or do something wrong?"

"You will have to ask her that, Cimarron. I can't say."

"Come on. She must have said something to you. What did she say? Tell me Mary Lee. I got to know what I did wrong that changed her mind. Do I need to apologize for something? What do I need to apologize for, tell me?"

"I really don't want your feelings to be hurt Cimarron. I guess your kiss scared her or something like that. At least that is what she said. She is afraid to be alone with you for fear you will have your way with her."

"Oh no. I guess I really did get into that kiss pretty heavy. She was turning me on. I owe her an apology. How do I get to your ranch so I can apologize to her?"

"I wouldn't advise you to go to the ranch after her. Our pa doesn't know I'm going out to lunch with Tyler. If he finds out no telling what he will do to Tyler. Let it go for now. I'll talk to her tonight. Maybe she will change her mind and go out to dinner with you one evening."

"I want to make it right with her, Mary Lee. I don't want it to just hang like this."

"I'm sorry, Cimarron. Give me a chance to talk to her and we will set something up again. I'll try and change her mind about you. Shall we go Tyler?"

"Yes, ma'am. See you later Cimarron. Have yourself a good *boring* day!" Tyler moved the team out and headed for the lake and a quiet picnic with Mary Lee."

Cimarron was fit to be tied. He was never stood up by a girl on a date before. It was a new emotion for him and he didn't like the feeling at all. It was bad for his ego. He was left in a quandary as to what to do about it. It would have been his first date with the daughter of a rancher. Most of his dates were saloon girls and they never refused his charms. Perhaps maybe he *was* moving in too fast on this real nice girl. Maybe he needed to take some lessons from Tyler on how to approach nice girls at an easy pace. He was too use to moving in fast on a girl because he never stayed very long in one place. Moving fast always got the acquaintance done in a hurry so he could advance the relationship at a speedy rate. Something went wrong somewhere. Perhaps he is losing his charm on wimmen. There was something really special about Jeanne that was making his head go crazy over this girl. This needed to be straightened out in a hurry.

As disappointed as he was, he was still feeling hungry. He headed to the Brotherhood Hash House to join TJ and Gage for lunch. He sat down at their table just as they were ordering so he ordered also.

"What happened, Cimarron? I thought you had a lunch date," said TJ.

"I got stood up; and don't laugh."

"You mean the lover boy of Yuma lost his allure and got stood up! Ha, ha ha."

"Isn't that what I just said? I also said don't *laugh*. I need to apologize to this girl and set things straight. Even if I have to present her father with six horses."

"How can I not laugh? That's the big joke of the year!" replied TJ. "As for the six horses. You would do better winning an Indian maiden with them. Ha, ha."

"Okay, boys. So the joke's on me; I struck out. There's always got to be a first time. Did you find the girl, Rosey?

"No. She's not back from a freight run as yet. I don't know where she is now. This is getting serious. Sundell needs her testimony for his trial if I'm gonna get him out of a hanging. Nobody seems to know where she has gone. According to the freight clerk, she went on a long delivery with her father and the clerk don't know when they'll be back. Our brother is in a really big jam."

"Can I go looking for them, track them, and bring them back for the trial?"

"You could if that clerk would tell me where they went. Can't even follow the freight wagon tracks because last night's rain washed them all away. We are at a dead end," said TJ.

"How's Sundell? Is he still ailing?"

"No. The fever's gone, the bullet wound is healing well. He is still all bruised up from the beating he took from the deputies and he looks like hell with that black eye. Otherwise he is okay. He always was a tough cowboy. He is anxious to get out of that jail. Wants to see his new horse Shadow."

"Shadow? What about us? When is that scoundrel of a sheriff gonna let the rest of us in there to see our brother?"

"You can't see him until the trial. He will only let me in there since I'm his attorney."

"Did you tell Sundell you can't find Rosey Denver?"

"Yeah. I did and he is real scared. He asked me if hanging hurts real bad. He's expecting to hang, poor guy. Doesn't think I can get him off. I have doubts about it myself."

"You got to get him off, TJ. Pa won't stand for one of us getting hanged."

"I know it. I'm scared too Cim. I already wired ma and pa to get here as fast as they can. It would help him a great deal if he saw them at the trial. They should be coming in on the stage in a couple of days."

"There's gotta be a way we can get him out of that jail."

"There is Cim. If he is sentenced to hang, we are breaking him out and heading for the border. No brother of ours is getting hanged when he is innocent. The only thing is, you three boys have got to do it and leave me out of it or I'll lose my attorney's license."

"Okay. Since you are the one with all the brains, you plan it out and we'll do it. At least we will have a Plan B if you can't get him off."

~~~ *T2 Brand* ~~~

Two o'clock that afternoon the second trial began. This time they tried John W. Powell who they all called "JW". JW was a good looking, clean shaven, young cowboy who took a liking to Sundell and created a friendship between them. He only joined the gang because he was out of cowboy work and broke. He needed a grubstake to keep himself alive until he could get another job as a ranch cowhand. He asked TJ if he would be his attorney and try to get him off with a lighter sentence. TJ agreed to help him out.

In his testimony he claimed Sundell had his way with Rosey. JW didn't know any differently. Sundell had them all fooled, even JW, with his scheme about himself and Rosey having a relationship. It was the only way he could keep her safe from the brutality of the gang members which included any interest in her on JW's part. However, as a favor to his friend Sundell, JW confessed to his attorney TJ and the court, that Sundell was not involved in the robbery of the Brotherhood National Bank. Also, that Sundell was not involved in the kidnapping of the girl or the murders in the bank. TJ was relieved that this credible witness cleared his brother of three serious charges against him. It saved Attorney TJ a lot of time on investigative work for those three charges.

"JW. At the time the gang picked up Sundell in that clearing, did you have any knowledge about the missing two thousand dollars in ranch money that was supposed to be on him?" asked TJ.

"No, sir. All I know is he didn't have it on him. But I can tell you something else about it."

"Go ahead, JW," inquired TJ. JW was going to tell the court something even TJ didn't know as yet. TJ was listening hard at what JW was about to say.

"Well, last night when we were in our jail cells, I overheard Dash whispering and arguing with Payson in the cell next door. They were arguing about the two thousand dollars that was missing. Dash was accusing Payson of stealing it out of Sundell's saddle bags and hiding it on the rest of the gang. He wanted to know what Payson did with the money because he didn't share it with the gang and Dash wanted his part of the split."

"Dash suspected Payson took the money? Why?"

"Well because Payson stopped at the dead horse on the way down the mountain, before he hooked up with us at the bank. He told Dash he searched the belongings on the dead horse and nothing of importance was there. That was before Sundell woke up and climbed down off the mountain's ledge to retrieve his stuff. We found Sundell sleeping in the clearing on our way back from the robbery."

"So Dash strongly suspected that Payson took the money before the robbery and hid it from the rest of you boys?"

"Yes sir. That's right."

"Your honor, I have no more questions for this man." TJ's mind was churning for more answers. He turned around and looked in the faces of his three brothers. He didn't have to guess what they were also thinking. They must find where Payson hid the ranch money before anyone else gets to it.

The trial continued on for another half hour and then a verdict was brought down from the jury. John W. Powell received one count of assisting a bank robbery because he was holding the horses when the Brotherhood National Bank was robbed. He did not murder anyone so the murder charges were dropped. He was charged with assisted kidnapping and one count of theft of the Canyon Diablo stage. He was sentenced to two years of hard labor in Yuma prison and upon release one year of probation to a law enforcement officer.

"Your honor," said TJ. "Would you release JW to me for the one year probation, sir? I'll have a job waiting for him on my ranch as a cowhand when he gets out."

"Okay, Attorney Lacey. I can grant that and I will write it up in the sentence paperwork for you."

"Thank you, your honor."

"JW please stand. You will be taken to Yuma Prison when the Tumble Weed Wagon arrives and you will serve two years of hard labor. You will then be released into the custody of Attorney Thomas J. Lacey for one year of probation and to work on his ranch, after which time you will be released and your debt to society will be paid. Do you agree to abide by the terms of your sentence?"

"Yes, sir. Yes your honor, I agree. Thank you so much TJ." TJ just smiled and shook hands with JW.

"Good luck to you, cowboy," replied TJ. "I'll see you when you get out."

CHAPTER IX

THE HARD CASES

"Cimarron did you find out anything on the where a bouts of Rosey and her father?"

"No, TJ. I even tried to charm the female employee in the freight office and that didn't work either. She wouldn't tell me a thing."

"Boy, Cim. You are really striking out with the women in this town. You need a change in tactics. Ha, ha."

"Don't get smart with me, Brother Lawyer. What are your plans for today?"

"First we got to meet the stagecoach. Ma and pa should be on it. I was able to get them a room at Mrs. Warren's Boarding House. It should be coming in to town in about an hour or more."

"Okay. I'm going down to the Livery stable for a while. I'll brush down Shadow. I also found out the mare in there named Stardust belongs to Rosey. Sundell gave it to her and I want to get a better look at that mare. That Sundell is slick. He used the mare to draw out Shadow so he could catch that stallion."

"I'm not surprised," replied TJ. "Sundell knows his horseflesh."

Their attention was captured by the rattling of the Tumble Weed Wagon coming up the street and arriving in town. The wagon stopped in front of the jailhouse.

"Come on boys let's all take a walk up to the sheriff's office," said TJ.

The driver climbed down and went into the sheriff's office. The two guards walked to the back of the wagon and unlocked the hasp. The driver and the sheriff came out escorting Greg Wills and J. W. Powell to the back of the wagon. Their wrists were cuffed and their ankles were chained as they walked sluggishly dragging their chains to the wagon and climbing in. TJ walked up to the wagon and put his hand through the bars patting JW on the back for reassurance. JW turned around from where he was sitting and looked at him.

"Behave and stay clean and you will be out in no time. Make sure you heed my words and I'll be waiting for you when you get out with that job offer."

"Okay, TJ. Thanks again for everything. You saved me a hanging. I owe you."

"You owe me nothing but to stay alive and get back to me in two years. I'm short ranch hands. So long, JW." The wagon pulled away rattling and creaking moving east out of town. TJ silently hoped the kid would stay clean and get out on time. He stood there in the street watching the wagon move away until his stare couldn't see it anymore.

"What are you thinking, TJ," questioned Tyler.

"You don't want to know, but I'll tell you anyway. JW will replace Sundell should I be unable to get our brother released and Sundell hangs." Cimarron, Tyler and Gage just looked at TJ in dead silence with very long faces. TJ was so right. The brothers didn't want to know what he was thinking.

~~~ T2 Brand ~~~

The hammering and construction of the scaffolding was making a lot of noise and attracting a crowd to watch the building of it. When TJ looked over that way at the platform his stomach rolled with pain. Three hangman's nooses were being set up. The bastards were planning on hanging all three men that were left. *They had tried and convicted the men already*, he thought. *What is this world coming too? What happened to 'a man is innocent until proven guilty'?*

The Overland Stage Line roared past the Lacey Brothers kicking up dust and teetering to a stop in front of the saloon.

"Let's go boys, ma and pa are here," said TJ. They hustled down the plank walk to the saloon to meet the stagecoach.

Cimarron helped his mother, Ricki, down from the coach and their father, the Nevada Kid, came out behind her. The stage driver threw down their luggage for the Lacey boys to catch. Hugs, kisses and handshakes went all around the immediate family. When Nevada looked at his oldest son TJ, his face was straight and solemn with no expression on it.

"Yes. Well. I'm doing the best I can Pa," replied TJ to the blank expression. "Let's get you set up in your room. Mrs. Warren is expecting you."

"I'll see you all later, TJ. I'm going down to that Livery stable," replied Cimarron.

"Okay, Cimarron. Meet us at the Hash House around five o'clock for dinner."

~~~ *T2 Brand* ~~~

Ricki Lacey was unpacking their bags and getting settled into their room when Nevada took a hold of TJ's arm pushing him towards the door.

"Let's go down to the jail. I want to see my son."

"The sheriff won't let anyone but me in there, pa. You're wasting your time."

"He'll let me in. Let's go."

TJ turned and looked at his two brothers, Tyler and Gage. "Help ma get settled and we'll be right back."

When they entered the sheriff's office they found him asleep in his chair with his feet on the desk. TJ quietly called to him and there was no answer just snoring. TJ called to him again. Nothing. The Nevada Kid, in his impatience, shoved the sheriff's feet off the desk onto the floor and the sheriff woke up with a start.

"What? What's going on here? TJ! What are you doing?"

"We want to see my brother and client, sheriff."

"You know the rules TJ. Only you are allowed in there and only for five minutes at a time."

"Sheriff. You don't understand. This man is our father, Tom Lacey and he wants to see Sundell."

"Tom Lacey, huh? So you are the notorious outlaw the Nevada Kid. I saw many a poster on you. If I'm right, you did five years in Yuma Prison. I'm not surprised that one of *your* offspring wound up in my jail on hanging charges."

"I did *seven* years in Yuma, sheriff. I paid my debt. As I understand it, my son is an innocent man and in your jail on false charges. You'll let me in there all right or you'll forever wish you had." Nevada's hand slid down close to his holstered gun. The sheriff looked down at Nevada's hand and changed his mind. This town didn't pay him enough to go up against a fast gun like the Nevada Kid.

"Well, I guess I can bend the rules just a little bit. Don't tell anybody I let you in. Leave your weapons here. But no more than five minutes in there."

TJ couldn't help but wonder why he didn't have the power to be as persuasive as his father was with people. He had his father's low voice, not as gravelly, and he lacked the reputation. That was it, it had to be the reputation with the Younger Brothers Gang that gave his father the edge.

The sheriff unlocked the cell.

"Pa! What are you doing here?" Sundell got up off the bunk. So did Payson and Dash Cogburn who came over to hang on the bars. Sundell put his hand out for a shake and Nevada took it, pulled him in and gave him a big hug instead. He let out a big sigh.

"Sundell is your memory back again? You remember pa?" replied TJ.

"I sure do. Guess I got all my memory back. I've been laying here trying to remember the past."

"Son are you trying to do something I was never able to accomplish?" replied Nevada.

"What's that pa?"

"Get yourself *hanged*!"

"Aw pa. I'm innocent of all the charges against me. They're gonna hang an innocent man. They convicted me when they arrested me."

"Pa I was able to clear him of all the charges except for rape of a minor. Canyon Diablo dropped the charges on him for assisting a stage robbery because they figured he would get hanged here in Brotherhood on the bigger charge. Anyway they got all their payroll money back."

"I didn't rape that girl, pa. I never touched her except for kissing her. Can they hang a man for just kissing a girl? She gave me her consent to kiss her."

"He did her all right. The two of us are witnesses. He had himself a good old time," said Payson looking through the bars of the next cell.

"He's lying pa. I faked it all. Ask the girl. She'll tell you. We planned it all to keep the low down crooks off of her!"

"You want to tell me how you *fake* the rape of a minor, son! I raised all my sons to respect women."

"I never touched her pa. I swear. Find Rosey and ask her. She'll tell the truth."

"That's my problem pa. I can't find the girl. She and her father run a freighting company. They are out delivering freight contracts and the clerk in the freight office can't tell me where they are right now."

The sheriff interrupted their conversation. "Your time is up boys. Let's go. Come on out of the cell."

"I want another five minutes," replied Nevada.

"Out!" said the sheriff. They moved out. He unlocked the cell and they left the office.

~~~ T2 Brand ~~~

The next day the trial for Dash Cogburn was held in the Brotherhood courtroom. Things did not go very well at all for Dash. Having been the leader of the gang and the one who made all the robbery plans, Dash found no one available to accept being his defense. He had to be his own defense. The cards were stacked against him. Wanted posters for him were all over the territory for previous robberies and murders. He was found guilty of one count of murder of a bank clerk in Brotherhood, one count of kidnapping a minor, and bank robbery. He was sentenced to hang by the neck until dead right after the trials of Sundell and Payson. He confessed to the judge and the sheriff that he was positive Payson stole the two thousand dollars in ranch money that Sundell was carrying back home to the Flying T2 Ranch. He also confessed that Sundell was picked up on the trail after they robbed the bank and Payson kidnapped the girl. The judge requested the sheriff to make a report of the statements and drop all charges against Sundell with exception of the 'rape of a minor' charge.

TJ was relieved that he had only one charge to defend on his brother now. However, that one charge was still a hanging charge in California. He had to find that girl. She was the only witness to Sundell's freedom. He was out of options to save his brother with the exception of the girl Rosey Denver.

Tomorrow would be Westley Payson's trial and the day after that would be Sundell's. He had only two days left before his brother would hang. He was at the end of his wits so he decided to ask the judge if he could be the prosecuting attorney for Westley Payson and the judge agreed. In order to find the stolen ranch money he would have to grill Payson up and down and inside out. Finding that ranch money would help prove Sundell's story that he was on his way home from a business transaction when his horse stumbled and fell off the mountain trail. Mike Hammer was a credible witness in that he gave the money to Sundell for the contract. The missing piece of the puzzle was Rosey Denver. Where was Rosey Denver and will she show up in time for Sundell's trial?

~~~ T2 Brand ~~~

The only Lacey family member missing at the breakfast table of Mrs. Warren's Boarding House was Cimarron. Nevada looked around at all his sons.

"Where is Cimarron?" he asked.

"Don't know. None of us has seen him yet this morning," said Tyler.

"I saw him last night," replied Gage. "He said he was riding to Brawley this morning to meet someone. Said he would be back in time for Sundell's trial."

"What the hell does he think he is doing? We got a serious family situation going on here. He can't be visiting girlfriends now."

"I'll bet he is going to see that Jennifer or Janice Russell at the Pinion Pine Ranch," said Tyler.

"He better not be going to see Janice Russell," said TJ. "Janice is my friend."

"You never know about Cimarron," said Gage. "He is still depressed that Jeanne, the rancher's daughter, stood him up for that lunch date. He hasn't gotten over that as yet."

"I'll deal with his hide if and when he gets back," replied his father Nevada.

"Now, Nevada. Go easy on him. You said yourself, boys will be boys," replied Ricki. "Besides it's only a day's ride to Brawley. He hasn't seen the girls in a long time. Don't be so hard on him."

"Ma is right, pa. You said yourself he is a spirit-boy. Cimarron was looking for an excuse to ride Shadow fast and give him a workout for Sundell," said Gage.

<center>~~~ T2 Brand ~~~</center>

The trial for Westley Payson was about to begin. The town's folk entered and took their seats. Westley was a very unpopular man. He was a loud, boisterous drinker, a card shark that cheated when he gambled, he was ornery to anyone that came near him and was rude and rough with the ladies in the saloons. His trial was longer than all the others because there were a lot of charges against him. Payson was the only one charged with kidnapping Rosey Denver since he was the one that dragged her out of the bank and put her on his horse. Dash gave that away when he was interrogated. He didn't want that charge pinned on himself. Dash also blamed Rosey's bruises and scrapes on Payson's rough treatment of the girl. TJ's questioning did not go easy on Payson. He uncovered the fact that Sundell and Payson were fighting over the girl. Sundell was protecting her from the harsh treatment of Payson. The judge and jury began to look a little differently at Sundell's case and were having doubts about how his involvement measured up at this point in the case.

TJ remembered what JW told him. JW overheard Dash, in the jail, coming down heavy on Payson as to where the two thousand in stock money was hidden. So TJ drilled Payson hard as to when he took the money and where it was hidden. Westley Payson wondered how TJ knew about that. Payson finally broke down and confessed that he took the money from the saddle bags and hid it in the hollow of a tree in the clearing near Musky River. TJ sent Tyler and Gage out to recover the money and bring the money back. Tyler and Gage returned with the money before the trial was over and gave the evidence to the judge. The judge filled out some paperwork and handed the money over to Thomas Lacey, owner of the Flying T2 Ranch fulfilling the contract Mike Hammer had with the stock contractor. Payson's trial brought out a lot of answers to questions that were hanging open.

The verdict came down hard and fast on Westley Payson. He was charged with the murder of two bank clerks, kidnapping of a minor, assault on a minor, and robbery of the Brotherhood bank. He was sentenced to be hanged by the neck until dead next to Dash Cogburn. The hanging was to take place immediately after the trial and sentencing of the last of the Cogburn gang, Sundell Lacey. Sundell's trial was set for the next day at one o'clock in the afternoon.

~~~ T2 Brand ~~~

Sundell was scared. Who wouldn't be scared if they were up on hanging charges and knew they were innocent. He longed to see his black stallion, Shadow, just one more time before the noose was set. The sheriff said no way, it's not allowed. This upset Sundell even more. He loved that horse even more than anyone knew.

"Hey Sundell. What do you want for your last meal? Anything you want. Even dessert," teased the sheriff.

"I don't want anything. I'm not hungry. I can't eat."

"The law says you get a good last meal. I'll bring you steak and eggs, and bacon."

"Suit yourself, sheriff."

Sundell's last meal was still sitting in the cell untouched when Sheriff Bridges and TJ came in to take him to court. Sheriff Bridges cuffed his hands and started to chain his feet when TJ stopped the sheriff.

"Leave his feet free, sheriff. He isn't going to run away. I'm with him. I don't want him dragging chains on his feet when he walks into the courtroom. Our ma will be in court."

"All right, TJ. I'll grant you your wish out of respect for you as an attorney."

"TJ, ma is here in court? Why? I don't want her to see this. It will kill her. I thought just pa was here."

"They're both here, Sundell. In fact, the whole family is here to support you."

"I can't do this." Sundell held back; he was so upset.

"Let's go kid." Sheriff Bridges pushed him towards the door of his office.

"Take it easy, sheriff. There's no need for that. Sundell will walk into that court with his head held high and me right next to him."

"Then let's go," replied the sheriff.

"The court is now in session with Justice Davidson presiding so will you all please stand." Everyone stood while the judge entered.

"Thank you ladies and gentlemen. You may all be seated," replied Justice Davidson. "I would like to make the announcement that it is the obligation of this court to provide sentence on the accused defendant Sundell Lacey. The charges being assault on a minor, including rape of the said minor. Let the proceedings begin." The judge sat down at his desk slamming the gavel down one time.

"Your honor as attorney to the defendant, I will bring Sundell up to the witness stand and swear him in."

"Proceed," said the judge.

After the swearing-in, TJ asked Sundell to tell his whole story. Start from the very beginning with the delivery of stock to Mike Hammer's ranch, the horse losing its footing on the high mountainside trail and how you fell, hitting your head on a rock, when landing on the ledge that jut out the side of the mountain. Sundell did as he was told and gave his whole story.

"When you hit your head, it caused you to have amnesia, forgetting everything about your past and the fact that you were raised on the Flying T2 Cattle Ranch in Yuma, Arizona. You didn't even know your name. Am I correct?" said TJ.

"That's correct," agreed Sundell.

"Your honor. I want the court to know the doctor here in town confirmed Sundell's amnesia upon his examination when Sundell was first brought in and locked in his cell. Through the doctor's care, Sundell has fully regained his memory."

"Go on with your story, young man," replied the judge.

Sundell continued on with the whole story as it actually happened leaving out the part where Rosey took off on Stardust for the Chloride General Store. His story was outlandish enough for the court to believe so he left that part out. Throughout the whole time he told his story, Sundell found he could not look at his father or mother for fear he would totally break down with embarrassment. He told how Dash ordered him and Rosey to hold their horses while the gang robbed the Overland Stage Line in Canyon Diablo.

The judge interrupted the story. "Sundell were you in love with Rosey Denver? What I mean is did you fall in love with the girl during her time of captivity?"

Damn, thought TJ. *I tried like hell to stay away from that kind of questioning.*

There was complete silence on Sundell's part. "Answer my question young man!"

Sundell looked at TJ. TJ shook his head yes and Sundell answered the judge.

"When I first met Rosey it was my first instinct to protect her from the gang."

"Did you fall in love with the girl?" the judge asked again.

"Yes, your honor. I did." A hum breezed through the crowded courtroom.

The judge looked hard over at TJ. *Damn it*, thought TJ, *he knew I was staying away from that answer.*

"Did you have desires for that young innocent woman? Did you want to make love to her, Sundell? I'll remind you that you are under oath and must tell the truth."

TJ closed his eyes and took a breath. When he opened them he looked at Sundell and shook his head no, don't answer that question.

"Yes. I desired her. I wanted to make love to her but I swear I didn't touch her."

Oh no, thought TJ. *He just lost the case for me. That answer will be used against him.*

"Any more questions, attorney Lacey?" replied the judge.

"Your honor Sundell said he didn't touch her and I believe him. I've known this boy his whole life. I grew up with him. He is an honorable man as are all the Lacey brothers. I implore you to believe the boy when he says he did not touch the minor girl. After all he is still under oath."

"If there are no more questions on the part of his attorney, I will provide sentence. Please sit down Attorney Lacey. Thank you. Will the accused prisoner please rise." Sundell stood up from the witness chair. "Sundell Lacey is there anything more you would like to say to the court before I pronounce sentence?"

"No, sir," replied Sundell. "Just get it over with."

"After due consideration this court finds Sundell Lacey—uh."

The door of the courtroom burst open fast, crashing with pandemonium against the back wall of the room. It startled everyone in the room as if it were a bomb going off and stopped the judge short in the middle of his sentence. Cimarron Lacey walked up the isle holding the hand of and leading a buckskin clad fifteen year old young women. Gasps were heard throughout the courtroom. Sundell was frozen as they approached the judge's podium.

"Young man you are in contempt of my court bursting in on a trial such as this. I demand the sheriff arrest you and lock you up."

"Hold on your honor. This here girl is Rosey Denver and she has some things to say to this here court before you pronounce sentence. We didn't ride the whole night all the way from Brawley for nothing." Cimarron looked at TJ who had the biggest grin on his face that you could imagine.

"Thanks, Cimarron. I'll take over from here. Your honor I'd like to present to you my last witness, the one I told you was missing. Sundell, come down from the witness stand and sit down. Rosey put your hand on the bible and I'll swear you in. Do you swear to tell the whole truth and nothing but the truth so help you God?"

"I do," said Rosey. "Why wasn't I told this trial was going on?"

"Let's make this quick, your honor. I ask you Miss Rosey Denver did the accused Sundell Lacey ever physically abuse you, improperly assault you, or rape you against your will and without your consent?"

"No he did not," replied Rosey. "Sundell had my consent to kiss me and we faked having a relationship to keep the outlaw gang from abusing me in any way. Sundell kept telling them nobody touches my girl."

"So did the charade work for you?"

"Yes it did. Westley Payson tried several times to abuse me and have his way with me. Sundell and Westley had several fights over it and Sundell won every time. Sundell saved my dignity many times from this very nasty man."

"How did you get all the scratches and bruises on you? Who did that?"

"Again, TJ that was Westley Payson. He went after me when Sundell was out in the canyon trying to catch Shadow. He roughed me up and I fell against the table in the cabin. That's how I got the black eye. JW came to my rescue that time. When Sundell got back to the cabin and found out, he and Payson fought it out over my honor. Sundell won again."

"How can you prove it to this court that you were not violated by Sundell, Miss Rosey? Can we take your word for it?"

"That's easy. I'm still a virgin. A doctor's exam can easily prove that. I'm willing to submit to it if the court wishes."

"Your honor. I rest my case. The rest is up to the court. Miss Rosey Denver states that Sundell Lacey never violated her and she is willing to subject herself to a doctor's exam to prove his innocence. What is the verdict of the court?"

"Will the prisoner please rise," said the judge. Sundell stood up for the second time with his cuffed hands crossed in front of him and standing in an at ease position.

"After due consideration this court deems the testimony of Miss Rosey Denver to be accurate and correct. The court will not subject her to a doctor's exam since she is still a minor. The court hereby drops all charges against the accused prisoner Mr. Sundell Lacey, however, the court feels since he was easily led astray by the Cogburn Outlaw Gang he will be placed in the custody of Attorney Thomas J. Lacey for one year and after one year of working on Mr. Lacey's ranch he will be set free on his own recognizance."

The Lacey family all stood up and cheered. They were all hugging Sundell and Rosey Denver as the judge left the room and the towns' folk left the courtroom.

"Cimarron. How did you ever find Rosey?" asked TJ.

"Well, you see I went back to the freight company clerk and asked her what the last stop was on the freight wagon run. She told me it was Brawley, California. So I saddled Shadow, since he was the fastest horse in the stable, and I told him this run was to save his master's life. Shadow flew to Brawley like the trade winds were behind him. I found Rosey and her father unloading the freight wagon in front of the general store. When I told them this trial was on, she agreed to jump on Shadow's back with me and get back as fast as possible to testify. Her father said he would take his time driving the wagon back."

"Unbelievable!" replied TJ. He turned and noticed the piece of paper that the judge was reading from was left on the desk. He picked it up and read it. It said, hang by the neck until dead for the rape of a minor. TJ crumpled it up quickly before anyone else saw it and put it in his pocket. He pushed his way in through his brothers to get to Sundell. "All right it's my turn," he said. He grabbed Sundell and gave him the biggest hug to Sundell's surprise.

The next day, the Nevada Kid and Ricki Lacey left on the stage to go back to Yuma. The five brothers mounted and walked their horses down the main street following the direction of the stagecoach. Sundell suddenly stopped in front of the Denver Freighting Company. Rosey was standing on the plank walk watching them go by.

"Hey Rosey, he said. I'll be back when you are of age and you better be wearing a dress and let your hair down too, because we're going on a picnic by the lake."

"Sundell Lacey I'm holding you to that promise. You wire me before you come so I can be ready."

"I'll wire you all right. You take good care of Stardust, you hear?"

"I reckon I will, Sundell. I'll love her to pieces. Bye Sundell."

"So long, tootsie, and thanks ma'am for saving me from hanging." After tipping his hat to her he cantered Shadow into a faster pace to catch up with his brothers on the trail.

Chapter X

BACK AT THE RANCH

The starlight on the plains was dim and quiet tonight. Sundell felt complete freedom being able to work and push cattle under the open sky. He felt as if he was a partner to the wind and the sun as he circled the bawling herd of cattle. He was thankful to be back working on the ranch. It was lucky for him that he escaped the harsh judgment of the law in Brotherhood, California. It was lucky, also, that his brothers found him in time before the hanging while he still was suffering from amnesia. It was even luckier that Cimarron found Rosey Denver to testify and clear him before the sentencing. TJ his attorney brother, was able to clear the false charges against him and the judge was lenient in giving him one year probation under TJ's watch on the ranch.

Sometimes the law can get carried away and be careless with the lives of innocent men. This time the law did right by him and judged him fairly. He was now as free as the eagle that circles down on its nest to feed its young, then stretches upwards again towards the heavens to continue living its life's tempo.

"Let's go Shadow. Let's run like the wind." They took off across the range land like a bird in flight and didn't stop until they were both panting and breathless.

Book Seven Summary

CHRISTMAS SLEIGH RIDE

(Tyler Lacey's Story)

It was Tyler Lacey's turn to gather the cattle and the strays in the upper mountain ranges and move them down to the lower meadows before winter set in on the Flying T2 Rough Stock and Cattle Company ranch. Tyler and his four brothers took turns being the line rider living in the line shack, one month at time, doing what a cowhand's work required. The Christmas holiday was approaching fast and Tyler was looking forward to finishing up the job and going back down the mountain to join his brothers and parents for Christmas dinner and the tree decorating at the big house. On his way down the trail he questioned why an old chuck wagon was coming up the cattle trail trespassing on the T2's upper range.

Calico Gunderson was on the way to her Uncle's Broken Arrow Ranch down near Smithville, Arizona with her brother Corey and her sister Ginger. She somehow made two wrong turns with her wagon and found herself lost and heading west up a mountain trail that was getting narrower as she climbed higher. Calico was trying to figure out how she could get the wagon and mule team turned around and going south, when a sudden and freak snow storm hit the mountain area stranding her and the children in the wilderness.